LOVE BY SUNRISE
SOLHAVEN FOREVERS
BOOK THREE

LIZ MARTINSON

This is a work of fiction. Names, characters, places, and incidents are products of the author's imagination or are used fictitiously and are not to be construed as real. Any resemblance to actual events, locales, organizations or persons, living or dead, is entirely coincidental.

Love By Sunrise, Copyright © 2023 Liz Martinson

All rights reserved. No part of this book may be reproduced in any form or by any electronic or mechanical means, including information storage and retrieval systems, without written permission from the author, except for the use of brief quotations in a book review.

WARNING DISCLAIMER: This collection is suited for Adults 18+ only. Stories contain sexual situations and adult language. All characters depicted are of legal age.

Book Cover Design ©The Cover Fling

INTRODUCTION

There's something about Solhaven—Solhaven and love seem to go hand in hand, so beware if you visit.

Laid-back Jake has sworn off commitment, but falls for business woman Emily. Sweet Claire wins over Daniel, who arrives full of despair. Lizzie lacks confidence and is helped through her angst by the mysterious gardener, Anton.

Perhaps it's the sea air? Maybe there's a kelpie keeping watch who likes to lend a helping hand?

Whatever it is, true love is found in the tranquil and beautiful coastal scenery of south Wales, with its secret coves and peaceful beaches.

You'll fall in love with Solhaven itself, and which couple will prove to be your favourite?

The series Solhaven Forevers is set in a small town in Wales, UK.

The books are written in British English.

CHAPTER 1

MAXIMILIAN, crown prince of Mondorra, hovered on the edges of a crowd of the country's rich and influential, all jostling politely to speak personally to his father, the king.

It was July, and it was King Alessandro's birthday, which had always been a day of grand celebrations, but the older Max had grown, the more he regarded it with boredom and cynicism. His face was stony as he kept in the background, trying to avoid being sucked into the sycophantic melee. What on earth was the point of all this? It was wrong, in his view, for people to seek favour in this way, with sugared words and gestures of bonhomie. Respect should be born from endeavour instead. He shook his head tiredly. There was so much he could do to change Mondorra, improve it, if only he was allowed.

Max's face lit up when he saw Lady Beatrix arrive with her parents. Everyone expected him to marry her, and indeed, his father had declared it as fact to a favoured few, but Max and Bea knew it would never happen. Good friends, they most definitely were, but they felt no interest in each other sexually. They refused to announce their engagement, despite being under pressure to do so by both sets of parents.

'Bea! At last. Good to see you. You're a breath of fresh air.' Max moved towards her and kissed her on both cheeks, taking her hand and sighing as he indicated the crowd with a nod of his head. Apart from himself and Bea, there was no-one younger than fifty.

'Your father enjoys it,' Bea reminded him gently.

'My father and anyone his age. But this sort of thing should be in the past. I was just thinking many are here simply because they fear loss of royal favour if they don't come. Papa needs to realise this whole court thing is an anachronism, as are the footmen dressed up in those clothes.' A sweep of his hand encompassed the men standing round the walls wearing precisely tailored uniforms, their hair all styled in the same way.

'I take it you're no further forward with your arguments to modernise?'

He gave her a withering look, one eyebrow raised, the corner of his top lip curling upwards in scorn. 'I fear not. He simply won't listen. Says I'm too young. He sees me as his child, Bea, who still needs looking after, and Papa knows best. But I'm a grown man who has some good ideas worth considering.'

'If you have such good ideas and are so passionate about implementing them, why all the recent headlines about your sailing, skiing, horse riding and wining and dining various women? Being the playboy?'

'What else can I do?' He shrugged. 'I refuse to hang around the court, condoning the current set-up. As for the wining and dining, none of those women touch me emotionally. I have more fun with you. I wish I could find someone special. At least then I could concentrate on falling in love as an occupation.'

Beatrix pursed her lips. 'You need a gainful job of some sort, my lad. Drifting round the way you do won't make you feel any better. Surely Alessandro will listen to your plans for reform some day soon? Can he not see how Mondorra is being left behind compared to the rest of Europe?'

'Tell me about it.' Max lifted his hand and started itemising by touching each finger. 'Our roads are a nightmare and could so easily be improved. Schools and hospitals need updating. Our internet and phone coverage need updating. We have to instigate a system where ability is recognised and rewarded. Encourage a bit of immigration, too, because our industry is waning. And as a royal family, we need to live more simply. You know all this as well as I do.'

Laying her hand on his arm, Bea sighed and shook her head. 'You know full well I agree, and many of our friends, too.'

'Papa fears if we do these things, the country will want to go a step further and rid itself of the monarchy. To be honest, if they did, I'd not weep too much. I could earn a proper living unfettered by all the protocols surrounding me. You tell me what I do at the moment isn't a gainful occupation, and I agree. I've tried asking my father to at least let me get a job, even if he won't let me rule.'

'You have?' Beatrix turned to smile at the servant, who had paused respectfully with a tray of delicacies, and shook her head. 'No, thank you.'

Max also shook his head, and the servant moved on. 'Of course I have.' He frowned slightly as he glanced at Beatrix. 'Several times. But I get the same answer—no prince of the country can be seen working for his living. Full stop. The end.'

A stentorian voice announced lunch was served, and the crowd edged into the sumptuous dining-room. The seating was formally arranged. Alessandro was at one end of the table with Helena on one side. Max was expected to sit at the other end, and he already knew Beatrix had been allocated the place next to him. It was Alessandro's way of subtly informing the court that Beatrix was to be Max's wife.

'Tell me how your refuge is progressing,' Max asked, as they both unfolded the pristine white serviettes and covered their laps.

Bea's face brightened. 'Oh, it's doing so well, Max. I've a rota of volunteers now, so we're fully covered in case someone needs our help during the night. The rooms are all decorated, and the nursery is ready.'

'Security?'

'All good. The women who come to us should feel safe. Now we have this one set up here in Alondra, my next aim is to start two more, one in St Prasse and the other in Lac Bienvenue.'

'I envy you the freedom to do such things.'

Beatrix took a mouthful of the starter, which the guests had been unable to touch until the king ate. Max hated the tradition, the pomp and the hierarchy of these occasions, and had expected the usual teasing comments from Bea about the wait. She must have sensed his dark mood, however, and refrained, for which he was grateful. Otherwise, he might have completely lost it and thrown his plate across the room.

'Yes, yes. I've more freedom than you. But not a great deal.' She shook her head again. 'There has to be something you can do, otherwise you're going to fall into the habit of being nothing but a dissolute playboy until the time comes for you to inherit.'

'I love my father and hope he lives a long time yet, but I'm so *bored*.' He kept his voice low, but he couldn't stop himself from banging his clenched fist on the table, which cut through the politely subdued chitchat like a bullet from a gun.

All eyes swivelled his way, and his father raised his eyebrows, looking mildly displeased.

Max waved a dismissive hand. 'My apologies. Please —go on. It is nothing of importance.'

Snorting inelegantly, Bea stifled a laugh. 'Hah! Nothing of importance? I think not, my friend.'

They continued in a similar vein throughout the meal until the last toast had been drunk and the coffee was served.

'I gather we've a treat in store this afternoon,' Bea murmured as she stirred cream into her cup and reached forwards for one of the chocolates sitting in front of them on a silver platter.

His face brightened, and for the first time since the whole day had started, Max smiled. 'Yes! The MetroCapital Ballet Company has made a special stop on their way home from their European tour. I suspect my father has paid them extra, because it looks good for him to have them perform for his birthday.'

Bea laughed. 'Oh, Max! You really are a cynical sour puss today. Perhaps they didn't mind a stop off here, if it's on their way home? What are they dancing?'

'Swan Lake.'

'Oh, lovely, a treat indeed. That's one of my favourites. I'm looking forward to this.' Beatrix stood up alongside Max and tucked her hand through his arm.

The king had already left the room, and people gradually filtered out after him. Cars waited on the large, gravelled forecourt of the palace, ready to drive them to the theatre. It was well within walking distance, but Max and Bea had no choice, and allowed themselves to be ushered into one of the waiting limousines. A driver and bodyguard sat expressionlessly in the front as they covered the short distance to the Alondra Theatre Royal.

The ballet promised to be superb. Lizzie Cassidy danced the role of Odette and Odile, and Bruno Bianchi danced Siegfried. Theirs was a well-known partnership, and Max looked forward to the performance as they settled into their seats.

The lights in the theatre dimmed, and the prince encountered the swan princess by a moonlit lake, Tchaikovsky's haunting music complementing the moves of the dance. When Max first saw Odette, the sudden shift in his chest, the cold wave which passed through him and took his breath away, surprised him.

Odd. He'd seen plenty of ballets and dancers, had spoken to them after the performance in his role as the crown prince, but never had he experienced feelings such as these, and they didn't pass, either, because, throughout the whole ballet, he felt on edge. It wasn't just her dancing that called to him. It was something else, as if all his life he'd been waiting for just this moment, for this woman.

Madness.

As far as he knew, having googled the company and cast before today, she was in a relationship with Bruno Bianchi, and had partnered him as a dancer since they'd first become members of the company.

He gasped, then quickly smothered the sound in his hand, as Bianchi appeared to stumble and Odette leapt nimbly back into a quick turn, before presenting herself to continue the pas de deux. A quick look round from the royal box showed him that no-one else seemed to notice, but he watched more closely from then on. However, Bianchi didn't slip again, and the ballet came to its tragically sad conclusion.

Max patted Bea's arm as she pulled a hanky from her tiny bag and sniffed into it. 'Oh! That was so beautiful.' She exhaled her breath. 'So, so beautiful. I never tire of Swan Lake, although I find many of the classical ballets a bit same-y now. I used to love them, but now I like more modern ballets.'

As they all rose to prepare for their return to the palace for the reception, which would include the ballet company, Bea continued talking. 'I was in Paris not so long ago and went to a show put on by the Dame Moulin company. It was an incredible mix of modern and some of the more traditional, too. One of their dancers was superb. I spoke to him at the sponsors' dinner afterwards. He was most enthusiastic.'

'Did you see him again?' Max grinned at her, an eyebrow raised.

'Hardly. We didn't get to know each other that well, and I was coming home the following day.'

But she looked wistful, and Max fleetingly wondered if she fancied the guy.

The reception was held after the evening dinner, in the magnificent ballroom of the palace, and they had invited many people. There was to be dancing, as well as meeting the ballet company. The meal and reception required evening dress, and Max pulled at his collar in irritation after being helped to dress to perfection by Jacques, who was his manservant. He was more than capable of getting himself dressed and hated the tradition which dictated he should have someone to assist. As a student at Cambridge, he'd had to wear black tie for formal dinners in hall and for the summer balls, and he'd had no-one waiting on him then. He'd rather enjoyed those few precious years as plain Anton Monsarrat, and had learned you didn't need to be a crown prince to gain friends or girlfriends. It was a lesson he carried with him always and made him cautious when he returned home. He was wary of sycophantic friendship, and women who maybe fancied being the crown princess but didn't fancy him.

He looked at himself in the mirror, his dark green, gold-flecked eyes glowering back, and ran his fingers through hair the colour of newly-shucked chestnuts, causing Jacques to roll his eyes.

'Yes, yes,' Max said, turning and giving the long-suffering man a grin. 'I know—you despair of me. I apologise, Jacques.'

Poor Jacques backed off, shaking his head. 'Your Highness looks fine. Maybe if you combed your hair again? No? Then I will bid you good evening, sir.'

He scuttled out and it was Max's turn to look resigned as he twisted his lips and shrugged. He was sorry he annoyed Jacques and knew it was a frequent occurrence.

The dinner was interminable and boring. Max chatted to Bea, thankful she'd been placed by his side again, and made occasional comments to other nearby guests, but he was grateful when it was time to move. Bea, being sociable, wandered off into the crowd, finding plenty of people to stop and chat with. She'd tried to talk him into coming with her, but he'd shaken his head, a stubborn set to his mouth which warned her off trying to persuade him.

He wasn't sure what was wrong tonight, but he didn't want to be included in the reception line and displayed as the Crown Prince. Instead, he lurked in the shadows, wishing he could leave, but knowing he couldn't because it would upset his father.

Something more held him there against his will, too. He wanted to see Lizzie Cassidy close up and work out what it was he felt for her and whether his emotion had only been caused by her dancing.

At last, she arrived.

Attempting to be detached and critical of her, he saw a slim woman with dark hair still pulled back into a bun at her nape, wearing a simple blue dress. There was nothing detached about the way his body responded to her, though. His heart picked up its beat, his mouth went dry, and his hands trembled. Something… there was something about her. For an insane moment, Max thought about using his position to be introduced, only to dismiss it immediately, feeling disgusted with himself. But what was he to do—stay here, and never know what might have been, or go over to meet her—in which case she'd know who he was?

At that very moment, she turned, and their eyes met. Her hand rose to her throat, her eyes widening. Then she froze, and he knew—*he knew*—she, too, was affected.

Simultaneously, her dancing partner pulled on her arm and whispered to her. She laughed, rather a brittle sound to Max's ears, and led Bianchi to his parents to be introduced. Max felt as though someone had thrown a cold bucket of water over him as she turned away. Relaxing back against his wall, he let out his breath and closed his eyes, re-living the moment when their eyes had met. He wanted to talk to her, but if he did, it would bring them both unwelcome attention.

Feeling a light touch on his arm, Max jumped. He opened his eyes and saw the very subject of his thoughts standing in front of him. Was he dreaming? Not by the very physical way his body was responding now she was close.

'Are you all right?' she asked, her voice hurried, an anxious look in her eyes as she flicked a glance over her shoulder.

Looking up, Max saw Bianchi, on the edge of the group round the king and queen, watching Lizzie closely, a glower on his face. The rumour that Bianchi was a demanding partner in all ways was true then, judging by his very jealous features.

He looked at her again, then dropped his gaze to her hand on his arm. Her sleeve had fallen back, and there was a ring of ugly redness turning fast to bruising around her lower arm, between her elbow and wrist. It looked fresh. He raised his head, shocked.

Lizzie glanced down, bit back an exclamation, and removed her hand. Her cheeks stained crimson as she again shot a glance behind her. This time Max most definitely could see anxiety and genuine fear, too, on her delicate features.

'I think,' he bit out between gritted teeth, a flash of atavistic anger shooting through him as his fists clenched, 'I should be the one to ask you that?'

'No, no. It's nothing. I hurt myself with my hairdryer. Th-the cord, you know…? But you… You look so sad?'

'I lack a purpose in my life.' He thought of his futile wish to improve his country.

They continued to stare at each other.

'Perhaps you should find one? A life with no purpose isn't good.'

'Perhaps,' Max replied evenly, '*you* should get a new hairdryer? If, that is, you get entangled with the cord frequently?' His gaze swept past her, toward Bianchi again, who was now frowning and shifting from foot to foot like a bull about to charge. Max wished he could snap his fingers and have him consigned to a deep dungeon, of which he knew there were many remaining, but he knew realistically it was impossible and allowed himself a small, wry twist of his lips.

Lizzie's eyes followed his. 'I must go,' she said breathlessly. 'I had to come over and speak to you, but I don't know why.' She stood for a moment, contemplating his face before repeating her words in a rather bewildered way. 'I don't know why. I can't stay. Not now. I must go!'

She whirled, her skirts flaring out round her slim legs.

'Change your hairdryer!' Max called after her in a soft voice.

Her steps faltered, her flight paused for a moment. She'd heard.

She turned and took a few steps backwards, replying in an equally soft voice. 'Find a purpose in your life!'

Within seconds, she'd returned to Bianchi's side, laughing up at him, smiling, patting his arm. The dancer allowed himself to be led away, still casting furious glances over his shoulder at Max, who stood and watched him impassively.

Eventually, Max turned and went outside onto the terrace where he stood, his hands braced on the stone coping, gazing over the gardens, listening to the fountains. He stood there for a very long time, thinking about Lizzie Cassidy and wondering about their strange attraction. Thinking also of their odd conversation, worrying about her relationship with Bianchi, and debating what he could do other than ask Bea's advice. She was good at that sort of stuff. Personally, he'd just punch the guy.

Her words, though, about a life with no purpose, and Bea's earlier chastisement about doing nothing but play these days, stuck with him.

He eventually went to his room and prepared for bed almost without noticing, his mind too full of his tumbling thoughts. Lizzie and Bea. His father. The country. His utter boredom with life as it was. He needed to make a stance and take some action. He had to make his father see it was time he played a much greater role in Mondorra. Max loved his country, and it hurt him to see its decay which could, so easily, be stopped.

But somehow he doubted he'd be any more successful than he'd been over the last few years since returning from university.

In which case, he decided, as he tossed and turned throughout the night, more awake than asleep, it was time to go. Find himself an occupation and hopefully shock his parents, his father especially, into realising just how useless and bored he felt, and how serious he was in wanting to be part of the ruling assembly.

It was an idea he'd dithered with several times, but one he'd always abandoned as being too drastic. Still, maybe drastic was needed.

The following morning, as he helped himself to his usual breakfast of muesli, fruit and yogurt, he listened open-mouthed to his father's declaration and knew his decision was right.

'You are nearly thirty-four, and it's time we had an heir. You will marry Beatrix in the August of next summer,' his papa pronounced. 'Her father and I agree it is a most suitable match. We shall announce it six months before, in February.'

His parents were loving, and his upbringing had been reasonable because as a family they'd spent time together at their country mansion and their seaside villa. It was only when it involved marrying Bea, running Mondorra, and modernisation, he and his father ended up with locked horns. Recently, the clashes had become too dominant, pushing their happier times into the distant recesses of his mind, threatening to wreck them as a family altogether, and making him resentful.

He caught the pleading glance from Helena, his mother. She was silently begging him to go along with Alessandro, but the time for that was long past, and shame overwhelmed him. He'd been too cowardly to force the issue before now. It had taken his best friend and the words of a stranger to spur him finally into action.

'Papa, I need you to listen. As things stand, I feel of no use at all—'

'Not so,' Alessandro interrupted. 'That is foolish. *You* are foolish. You are my heir and you need to learn how to run the country by my side.'

Oh, *fuck*! This hadn't been a straightforward decision to make, and it deeply saddened him it'd come to this.

'Please, Papa. I mean it. I shall leave straight after breakfast. I haven't made this decision lightly, but it's been at the back of my mind for some time now. This is your last chance to agree. I think I understand, maybe more than you, the needs of our country in this century. Mondorra is falling further and further behind the rest of Europe. We need to effect change—a lot of it.'

A long silence followed.

Max stood and went to kiss his father's cheek and then his mother's. 'I'm sorry. So very sorry it has come to this, but I cannot go on as I am. I need a purpose in my life.'

Oh, Lizzie Cassidy, little do you know your words lit the fuse. He gazed at his parents sadly, knowing his father would find it impossible to back down. Some time apart might actually help. Certainly help Max, for he intended to work. But maybe it would give his father breathing space and a way to back down gracefully.

He surely hoped so.

As his father gazed at him, mouth open and eyes wide, and his mother wrung her hands and wept, Maximilian Anton de Casimir, Prince of Mondorra, gave his parents a small bow, and quietly left.

CHAPTER 2

Lizzie Cassidy bent into a plie, back straight, chin raised, a calm smile on her face. She gracefully extended her arm to the side while her other hand lay lightly on the barre.

The daily class was just starting, and, as she did every day, she welcomed the safety of the ballet studio and the mindless repetition of moves and exercises she'd been building and repeating since she'd had her first ballet lesson at the age of five. After the barre work, the class would move onto the floor. There, she relished the stretch and pull of her body, and the further shutting down of her thoughts, as the ballet master called commands. The thump and shuffle of feet, and the beat of the piano chords, led her effortlessly through, from barre to floor to the final curtsey. It was a time of self-introspection and peace. Oh, yes… peace. Unbelievable and unexpected *peace*.

Peter Wellesley, the senior ballet master, dismissed the class and beckoned to her. Stepping gracefully over the shining floor, a towel slung round her neck, water bottle in hand, she joined him, a slight look of surprise on her face.

Surprise which grew when the studio doors opened and the director entered, alongside a stranger. He was obviously a dancer, because he was in practice clothes. He hadn't been in class, although the sheen of sweat on his face showed he'd been working somewhere else. He was tall, his very dark brown hair swept back from his forehead, although a heavy lock kept falling forward, which he sometimes shook back. His eyes were too far away for her to see their colour. Lizzie wondered who he was and why he was there. If it was as a potential partner for her, it would be a surprise, for she was familiar with most principal dancers in Europe, and even a few in the Americas, and this one was a complete unknown.

'Lizzie.' The director, Harry Graves, nodded at her. 'Peter.'

Harry and Peter moved into a huddle and exchanged some low-voiced words. The dancer stood calmly near the barre over by the far windows, looking round at the studio, at her, and at the two men. Apart from herself, they all seemed to know what was going on.

Eventually, Harry pulled away from Peter and took her hand in his, searching her face. 'How are things these days?'

'I'm good,' Lizzie mumbled, looking down at her pointe shoes and tracing a pattern over the parquet with one toe.

'Bruno keeping away from you? Have you seen him hanging around? Here, or your sister's house?'

'No.'

'Mmm, good.' was all Harry said in response.

She knew he was sympathetic. Everyone was.

Bruno Bianchi, darling of the ballet world, and her partner for twelve years, had finally lost everything as, indeed, so had she.

Spurred on by the comments of the sad man she'd talked to in Mondorra six months ago, Lizzie had finally found the courage to leave Bruno, and, once back in England, had moved in with her sister and brother-in-law.

Shortly afterwards, Bruno lost his place in the company. Turned out they'd been very aware of problems in the dancer's life.

For years, her life had been the stuff every young girl dreams about—to be the principal dancer with an extremely handsome prince dancing alongside, eventually moving in together, the golden couple of ballet, and being happy ever after.

But it had ended up more nightmare than dream, for various reasons Lizzie had never yet found the courage to talk about. That, plus the stress of losing her partner, no matter his faults, and the threats he'd shouted at her as he'd walked out of the door on his last day, had all affected her dancing. She'd lost her emotional input and, to some extent, her confidence in performing, although technically she was still one of the best.

She wanted to regain it all.

Startled, Lizzie realised Harry was speaking to her again. 'I'm sorry?'

'We have an idea, Peter and I, plus some others involved in your return to dancing.'

Lizzie looked from Harry to Peter before allowing her gaze to settle once more on the unknown dancer who was now gazing out of the window, having tactfully turned his back on this part of the discussion. 'And your idea is?'

'I don't think you'll disagree when we say your technical brilliance remains, but your emotions have been under great strain. Understandably so, understandably so. But we need to get you back as you were, with joy, fire, sadness. With your heart, dear one. With your *heart*.'

'I try.' Lizzie frowned, pressing her lips together. Despite knowing this, it hurt to hear it so baldly put.

'I know, dear girl. But you haven't created a bond with another partner yet. We think when you do, your spark will return. Forget Bruno and what you once had together. Forget what he's become. If you don't, he'll drag you down as well. Do you want that to happen?'

'No, I don't.' She sat down in one of the chairs grouped round the piano, unable to stop her sulky expression.

Peter patted her arm as he joined her. 'Cheer up.'

'I know full well if our roles had been reversed, Bruno wouldn't have allowed himself a moment's worry, or blamed himself, and would've replaced me as a partner in the blink of an eye,' Lizzie murmured.

'Quite. So you must replace him, because we think

you've still got a lot to offer. We'd like you back, and with a new partner.'

Aware of Harry and Peter exchanging another look, Lizzie bought some time as she scrubbed her hands over her face before wiping them on her practice clothes.

'Have you seen the company counsellor?' Peter asked her gently.

'You know I have. And you probably know exactly what transpired between us!' Inside, she shrivelled and hoped that wasn't true. The counsellor would probably tell them that getting her to open up was proving extremely difficult.

Yes, it would be good if she could let everything out. But she would have to trust someone completely before she bared her soul, released her fears, and not just babbled on about guilt and relief and other vague things as she'd done so far in her sessions.

A man's face floated into her mind. A man who'd looked tired and ineffably sad as he'd stood on the fringe of the glittering reception, keeping to the shadows. Something about him had called to her, and despite Bruno's glowering presence, despite her trepidation at what he might do later, alone in their hotel room, Lizzie had gone over to speak to him. It wasn't the place to talk for any length of time, so it was just as well he'd kept it short. But what he'd said had stuck and finally convinced her to give up on the relationship. He'd stayed with her ever since, and if she ever met him again, she felt he was someone she could trust. Pity it was so unlikely ever to happen.

Harry looked shocked. 'That's confidential, Lizzie, and hurtful you should even suggest we might.'

After a few beats of silence, Lizzie shifted in her chair. 'Okay, okay. I'm sorry. Look, let's get back to dancing. I know I'm technically still good, but yes, I also know I'm holding back when I'm dancing with someone. Well, lacking heart, as you said. Won't that *do*?'

'I repeat… after what you gave us before?'

Another long silence followed.

Lizzie linked her fingers together. 'Okay. So now what? What's this idea of yours?'

Harry's face lit up with enthusiasm. 'You know about our outreach programme?'

Of course she did. The entire company approved of it. Cells of dancers went out and based themselves in areas for two months at a time. They gave talks, demonstrations, performances, and welcomed visitors to their classes. Lizzie and Bruno had both been part of such groups in the past, but as MetroCapital never sent their top principal dancers, neither had gone in recent years.

Almost reading her thoughts, Harry explained. 'I know someone of your stature within the company wouldn't normally go. Of course, you can say no to our suggestion, but we wondered if you might relax away from the spotlight. Away from the pressure of dancing here in London, where you and Bruno have always danced together and everyone is watching to see how you'll perform without him. If you went with another high-calibre dancer, you might build a new partnership in a more relaxed atmosphere. Once you have a new partner, we think you'll be able to move forwards.'

'It's a lot of ifs and maybes, Lizzie,' Peter added. 'We know that. But we truly want you back. You're one of the greats, and as Harry just said, you've got so much more to offer the world yet. Don't let Bruno defeat you.'

Lizzie noticed the man over by the windows had turned and was now regarding the small group, his face devoid of expression. At a nod from Harry, he crossed the room with a lyrical grace, pulled a chair towards him and reversed it, sitting leaning with his forearms across the back, his legs straddling the seat.

'This,' said Harry, with the air of someone successfully pulling a rabbit from the hat, 'is Tim Faversham. He's from France, despite the British name. His mother is French, and they moved over there when he was eight. He's a late-comer to ballet. Started early with theatre dance, with some ballet on the side, of course. He did some serious ballet training when he was sixteen, then left school to attend a dance and drama college. One teacher there spotted his talent for ballet and persuaded him to concentrate on that, but Tim insisted he wanted to continue with all the other types of dance, so he's a bit of an all-rounder. His whole training is unconventional from a classical ballet point of view, and he's never worked with a ballet company, been in a corps, or had solo roles.' And then, after a pointed few seconds, 'Or regularly partnered anyone.'

Lizzie glanced at Tim Faversham, who raised an eyebrow and gave her a faint smile. 'Bit damning, that, *n'est-ce pas?*'

His accent was non-existent and his eyes were grey.

'You're bi-lingual?'

'Most definitely. My papa insisted we all spoke English one day, French the next, from being tiny.' His smile widened.

'Lizzie, meet Tim. Tim, meet Lizzie Cassidy, one of our top principal dancers.' Harry looked from one to the other.

Once he would have said "our top principal dancer", but she knew without Bruno her standing had dropped, despite him being the transgressor. Not a lot, but definitely lower now.

'Hello, Tim. I suppose you're *au fait* with my history?' Her mouth lifted in a half-smile as she threw the French words in.

'*Bien sur*. We're the bad boys, you and me. Me because I lack the classical ballet company discipline and experience, and you because you're sad and can't rediscover your joy of dancing. I've seen you with Bruno, in Paris, about three years ago. You were *tres magnifique*.' His face was serious as he looked at her with narrowed eyes.

'Okay, okay, okay!' Harry threw up his hands. 'Enough with the French phrases. We get the idea. And yes, you're right, Tim. She was indeed magnificent in Romeo and Juliet. So okay, Tim has maybe summed things up rather neatly there—you're both the bad boys. But I wouldn't use that term. Tim, yes, you lack the experience of a company and a partner, and Lizzie, you're going through a bad patch emotionally. So we thought why not send you both off together on a two month outreach? You can learn to dance a few roles together and use them for your demos. Tim, maybe you could use some of your other talents when you go into schools. The theatre dancing? Tap, maybe? The marketing and promotion departments are working out your itinerary, but we thought we'd base you in one place and you could travel out from there by coach.'

'Where,' asked Lizzie patiently, 'are you sending us?'

'Wales. It's been some time since we went there, and a couple of small theatres have asked us to go back. Peter is drawing up a programme of pas de deux and excerpts from the more popular ballets. I repeat, I know it's unusual, sending someone of your standing, but we think it might let you get some enjoyment out of performing without all the pressure. Would you be happy to go? We're looking at July and August, so a real holiday period for everyone. There will be some time at weekends to enjoy the local beaches. Maybe even the occasional day-off mid-week, but we often find people contact us once they know we're in the area and asking us to slip things into the itinerary.'

'But I've only just met Tim. I don't know what sort of dancer he is. Sorry, Tim,' Lizzie said, turning to him with apology in her voice, 'but I need to know, before I commit to partnering you for two months. Your training sounds a bit off the grid. I'm not sure it would be wise for us to rely so much on each other, even doing outreach. You might not be up to my standard or used to lifts or—'

'Shh, Lizzie,' Tim said, rising to his feet. 'Come on,

let's try something simple, shall we? Maybe the wedding pas de deux from Coppelia?'

'You know it?'

He laughed and shook his head. 'Have some faith in Harry and Peter. They've vetted me, and it's them who asked me to come here, not me who came cap in hand, okay?'

He held out his hand as the pianist tried a few chords, nodding quietly to himself.

'The lifts?' Lizzie's voice was apprehensive, her hands, hidden by her sides, trembled, and her stomach lurched with uncertainty. She'd lost the ability to trust her own skills—Bruno had eroded her confidence with his scathing comments, told her repeatedly it was all her fault—and she also found it hard to give herself completely over to any new partner since his erratic dancing in the year before he left had left her afraid.

'Trust me?'

Lizzie stared apprehensively into his grey eyes and rose reluctantly to her feet. Maybe the board was right. Get away from the memories of Bruno and the disintegration of their love and partnership. Get away from London. It would be a sort of holiday, and she'd be able to stop looking over her shoulder. She'd be able to relax.

But trusting him would be very hard.

CHAPTER 3

ANTON MONSARRAT, known in Mondorra as Prince Maximilian de Casimir, felt amused. Not merely because he was using the old name he'd used when he'd been a student at Cambridge, but because of his current situation.

He looked round the room he'd been offered as part of the package for his new job as the under gardener at Haven House Hotel. Yes, as well as this small room, his new job title entertained him, too—under gardener! Bea would love it and also love the fact his boss was a woman. His parents, however, wouldn't find it at all funny. That he was deranged would be foremost in their minds.

There was nothing wrong with the room. It was airy, bright, and clean, and it contained a double bed, an easy chair, a microwave and a kettle. Tucked into one corner was a compact ensuite. There was a skylight and a window overlooking the courtyard, which seemed fairly quiet. His access was through the large garage, where the hotel kept a couple of golf buggies and, he presumed, the owners' vehicles. He liked the private access, guessed the space had once housed carriages and his room had been part of the hayloft.

No, nothing wrong with it at all.

Just that it was… small.

He'd not met the owners of the hotel yet because he'd been interviewed last week by the head gardener, Ms Bradstock, who was pregnant. She'd told him he'd have to be in full charge for around three months after her baby was born in March. Then she'd asked if he thought he had the experience for such responsibility because they were going to start a massive restoration project to return the gardens to their Victorian splendour.

Hmm. Still looking round, he rubbed his chin, shadowed with stubble, in need of a shave. If he'd answered truthfully, he would have said no, he didn't have the experience. However, with many years spent learning from a gardener at home who said he was a natural, plus a considerable interest in the environment, and a degree in economics from Cambridge, he'd decided it was something he could do. So, with great confidence, he'd said yes.

Nobody's fool, Ms Bradstock had eyed him thoughtfully and suggested he was maybe not the usual type for a gardener, and was he prepared to commit to at least a year, unless he proved unsuitable? He'd silently agreed with her summation, even though he'd felt uncertain about committing to the year she'd asked for. However, he knew he'd prove quite suitable, so he'd answered with another confident yes. As well as telling her he'd been employed in a French vineyard for the last six months, too, which seemed to surprise her, especially when he presented her with a written testimonial from the vineyard owner.

When she'd started in on more casual chit-chat, like where he came from, did he have any family, and what had he been doing before his job in the vineyard, he remained silent, and although he offered an apology, promising he could provide more references, he'd suggested personal topics were out of bounds.

Which had caused her to look startled before she'd nodded and agreed, her hand touching her baby bump.

Anton crossed to the window, opened it, and leaned against the wall, welcoming the cold air flowing through the gap. He stuffed his hands in the pockets of his jeans and gazed across the yard at the hotel. Coming to Solhaven had been deliberate, but choosing to stay surprised him.

He'd last been here eleven or twelve years ago, when he and a group of friends from Cambridge had come to surf for two years in a row. Back then, Solhaven was well-known in the surfing world as the home of Jake Bradstock, who although very young, was rapidly making a name for himself. Like groupies, they'd hoped to bump into him. It hadn't happened, but he'd remembered the place as being beautiful, with a couple of great surfing beaches, one of which had a decent café offering cheap, plentiful, and very good food.

Anton smiled. The waiter there had been a wannabe surfing type, easily remembered even after all this time.

His hair had been long and blonde, a riot of curls, and several times Anton had noticed him gazing rather wistfully out of the window at the action on the water.

Ms Bradstock—mmm, interesting. The same name as the surfer. Anton straightened, pushing himself away from the wall. Did she know Jake Bradstock? What had happened to him? He knew the surfer had eventually earned the title of world champion at least once. Max didn't know much other than that. Other things had dominated his life, and Solhaven had gradually faded from his memory only to pop back into his mind when he was wondering where he could go, once he'd finished at the vineyard.

He badly needed somewhere he'd been happy, and the two holidays he and his friends had taken down here had been very happy.

A month each time. Carefree and joyous days spent surfing, evenings spent in the locals pubs. The first campsite had been behind one of the surfing beaches, which was great, but they'd all decided they preferred Silver Sands, so the following year they'd located another site, with only a short walk needed to reach the beautiful beach.

But enough of the past and his holiday memories. Having left Mondorra, a hard stint of physical labour working the in the vineyard had helped him get rid of his frustration and anger, then memory had led him back to Solhaven. Once here, he'd seen the job advert in the local newsagent. It had also, Ms Bradstock told him, been advertised on a couple of online sites, but he suited her better than the other applicants.

This would be another complete change for him, but it would be good. Despite the prospect of more hard, outdoor work, which in mid-January might well prove cold and miserable, he suspected he'd enjoy it. He'd always loved gardening, cherishing plants, helping them develop.

He wanted to do the same for Mondorra—cherish it, nurture it, help it develop. Unable to do so, he'd left all he held dear, but some time away from his father and the court had seemed a good idea. There was much to be gained from fending for himself, and hopefully he'd shocked his papa into realising his ideas for the country had merit. Then he could go home and do the job he was born for.

Anton sighed. He wasn't sure what would happen if he finally returned home and his father still held the same views. There would be no grand gesture left for him if that was the case, other than threatening to abdicate—if that was possible? You could abdicate from being king, but from being crown prince? Mmm. It would cause a constitutional uproar and anyway, it wasn't something he wanted to do.

Pushing himself off the wall, he closed the window. He was hungry, and Ms Bradstock had promised him his meals were part of the contract, so he decided to go over to the hotel and join her, as she'd suggested. She intended to run through what she wanted to achieve over the coming year while they ate and give him the dates she expected to be out of circulation Although, as she'd pointed out, she would always be there for him to query something should he be in doubt. He rather liked the idea of a complete restoration of the grounds to how they were when the house was built, but that was a very long term project. As Ms Bradstock had said, there was plenty of work to be done on a day-to-day basis, too. Closing the door, he took the steps two at a time and soon found himself in the warm, beautiful Victorian dining-room.

Ah, and there was his boss, Ms Bradstock. Crossing the room, he pulled out the chair opposite and sat down with a nod of greeting.

'Anton, hello. Or do you prefer Mr Monsarrat?'

'Anton is fine.' Which, considering he'd never been called Mr Monsarrat, except occasionally in Cambridge, was a genuine response.

'Happy with your room?'

'My room is pleasant. It has all I need, and sometimes I can eat here, as you've mentioned.'

'Not sometimes.' Claire picked up her serviette, giving him a quick look. 'Anytime. All the time, if you want.'

'Then I shall become fat.' Anton grinned.

Ms Bradstock paused from putting the serviette on her lap, her mouth dropping slightly as she stared at him.

It often happened. His smile, so he'd been told, was… captivating.

'Not with the work I'll expect from you,' she replied with a half-smile. 'Call me Claire, by the way. Ms Bradstock reminds me too much of my previous career.'

'And that was?' Anton mirrored her actions as he took his own serviette and laid it in his lap.

'I used to teach. I loved the kids, hated the record keeping. And I wanted to come home to Wales and work outside.'

'Oh, my, a lot of change for you there.'

Claire sipped from her water glass. 'I suppose so. It certainly took determination to achieve what I really wanted from my life. I did a degree in horticulture over three years, studying part-time, gained work-experience in the holidays, and had just qualified when this job came up. I was brought up in Solhaven, so I was delighted.'

Looking thoughtful, Anton filled a few moments of silence by filling her glass, and then his own, with water. He admired her for what she'd done. Her words echoed in his mind—*determination to achieve what I really wanted from my life*. That had always been his ambition, too, but unlike Ms Bradstock—no, she'd said Claire—he'd achieved nothing much so far, except his degree and standing around at state functions like a window dummy; immaculately urbane, immaculately tailored, and unfailingly polite.

Well, that was so far. He was still determined to achieve the modernisation of Mondorra and the monarchy, but he'd put those ambitions on hold, because not knowing what else he could do, he'd deserted the battlefield. One day, he still hoped leading his country into the twenty-first century would be his greatest achievement.

There was a slightly uncomfortable thought lurking in his mind that the uncomplicated life of a gardener might be preferable. At least he'd have the complete freedom to let this place grow and change how he wanted. Did it mean he would give up on his country, his duty, his wishes for how he wanted Mondorra to develop for ever? No, very unlikely, but… giving a quick shake of his head he took a mouthful of water and noticed the questioning look on Claire's face, no doubt caused by his silence. Enough, before she got too serious.

Anton leaned forward. 'If you are a local person, and especially with your name, you must surely be able to solve something for me. About twelve years ago now, I came here on holiday twice. We were a group of friends from university, and we camped directly behind a good surf beach one year—'

'Howgale?'

'Yes! But we found Silver Sands, so the following year we camped near there. We came for the surfing, yes? One of our group was a very keen surfer, and he told us about a local boy who was an up-and-coming star—Jake Bradstock, the same name as yours.'

'Ha! Yes, I know Jake. He's my brother.'

'Really? I wondered if there might be a connection. I think we all hoped we'd meet him and maybe he would demonstrate for us. We never did, but I followed his career for a while before other things took precedence, and…' Anton broke off, eyes widening.

A man had walked over to their table and, thumbs hooked into his jeans' pockets, stood smiling at them both. Anton shook his head in bewilderment. This, surely, was the same lad who had waited on in the café at Silver Sands. Twelve years or more might have passed, but there was no mistaking the hair, the wannabe surfer look of the man even now, except he was dressed in jeans and a thick sweater rather than shorts and tee shirt.

Anton looked curiously from Claire to the man and could see a definite likeness. Was this her brother, then? Could it be possible the long-ago waiter had been the golden up-and-coming boy of the surf scene, in front of their noses the whole time?

'Um… you were talking about Jake just then?' Claire was asking him. Her eyes crinkled with amusement.

Anton gave a faint smile. 'Indeed I was, yes. And about to ask if you knew him and what had happened to him. But… it's even more strange than that. I remember a server in the café and thought at the time he looked as if he wished he could be out there with the surfers. Forgive me, but he was pretty unforgettable, with his hair. And now, here you are!' Anton snapped his fingers, shrugged, and leaned back. 'And I think you must be Jake Bradstock.'

The guy sat down and leaned his forearms on the table. 'Ha! Yes, I'm Jake. And yeah, I would've been wishing I was out there, that's definite. But I had to work as well. I often did my surf practising at dawn and again, much later after the café had closed.'

'This is amazing that we should finally meet. Well, well, well. We were groupies, you know. I was telling Claire, we came on holiday to surf, and we hoped we might meet you. I have sometimes wondered what became of you over the years.'

'Given up competitive surfing, settled down with a

beautiful partner, and I'm a father, too. Hey, you're not English, are you?'

There was a brief silence before Anton spoke, his words slow and deliberate. 'No. No, I am not. Is it so very obvious?'

'The way you speak is formal, and you've got a slight accent.' Jake shrugged carelessly. 'Are you staying here, then?'

Anton looked at Claire.

She laughed. 'He's the new gardener! Don't you remember I told you I'd interviewed last week?'

'So you did. Okay, new gardener, welcome. What's your name, then?'

'My name is Anton Monsarrat.'

Jake reached out his hand and shook Anton's. 'Hi.'

'This hotel is yours and your sister's?'

'Not mine,' Claire interjected hastily. 'I'm an employee, like you. Answerable to Emily. She's the one who runs the hotel. Jake still has the café.'

Anton felt slightly bewildered. 'Café? Emily?'

'The beautiful partner I mentioned.' Jake grinned at him.

Quickly, brother and sister gave Anton a potted history of the years between his camping holidays and the situation now.

When they'd finished, he gave a relieved smile. 'That is now good. I understand it all. I'm so sorry your career ended before you'd hoped, Mr Bradst—'

'Jake. And this is Claire, and when you meet Emily, she's just Emily, too. She's busy with the baby. She's called Olivia, and she's only three months old.' His eyes shone with pride as he spoke of his daughter.

'My congratulations.'

'So, think you'll like it here? How did you get into gardening, anyway?'

Two questions he could answer fairly easily. 'I see no reason I should not like it, and I've been following a gardener around for years, learning from him "on the job", I think is how you put it, yes? I've sent him an email, and he's going to send a reference for me. His name is Hansel.'

He'd used a generic email address rather than the hotel one and hoped Claire wouldn't query that. He couldn't trust Hansel not to take pity on his mama and tell him where he was to be found.

Claire nodded and took another sip of water. 'That's okay. Now, do you both want to order something? I'm starving.'

'Not for me. I'm not stopping. I saw you as I was passing and thought I'd just drop by to say hello. It's time to give Emily a bit of peace and take over bath time for young Olivia.' Jake stood and pushed his chair in, his entire face lighting up. Anton could see he was very much in love, and very proud of his family.

He felt envious. One day, he hoped he could look like this because of a woman, and hopefully, a child, too.

And here it came again, pirouetting into his mind—the cameo of the dancer, Lizzie Cassidy. He huffed at his stupidity and turned his attention to the menu. Not too bad, he thought, skimming down the main courses. Not too bad at all.

It looked as if his impulsive decision to return to a place he had such good memories of, followed by his second very impulsive decision to find employment while he was here, might prove enjoyable—and it would certainly be an excellent way to clear his mind.

Maybe he could even try to find Lizzie Cassidy one day, too.

CHAPTER 4

LIZZIE STARED out of the coach window as they left the main road and meandered through lanes lined with hawthorn, the verges bursting with campion and white daisies, which added their colours to the vibrant greens of grass and fresh leaves. This was a truly lovely place, and July was possibly the most ideal month to be here. She wasn't sure she'd ever been to this part of Wales and looked forward to seeing the sea, maybe walking on the beach. Haven House Hotel hadn't sounded very inspiring until she'd told her sister and brother-in-law, who'd surprised her by throwing back his head and laughing.

'What?' Lizzie had asked crossly.

'I was the architect for the place when they converted it into a hotel. The owner's brother is a friend, and he recommended me. That's quite a coincidence, your group staying there. It's a very beautiful place, Lizzie.' His face had sobered. 'It's very beautiful,' he'd repeated. 'It's a healing sort of place. And

Emily and Jake are great people. They won't fuss you. Say hi, won't you?'

When she finally checked it out on the internet, she discovered Solhaven was one of those sleepy seaside towns—well, almost a village, really—which offered very little apart from a glorious coast, some of the best beaches in Great Britain, and good food, ranging from cafes and gourmet fish and chips to highly recommended seafood restaurants She'd become enchanted and excited about her upcoming outreach.

Some beautiful seaside, daily classes and the occasional demonstration, talk or performance might be a good way back for her, and pleasantly relaxing, she admitted, as the coach turned into a tree-lined drive. Maybe Harry and Peter had been right in their suggestion that if she left London, where she'd done most of her dancing with Bruno—she shuddered—the lack of pressure would release her emotions.

Maybe.

Or maybe she'd continue as she was. A locked-down maelstrom of misery and fear, unable to fully trust another partner again in case what Bruno had told her was true—she was unable to dance without his support. It was this uncertainty which had caused her to lose all the confidence and joy in her dancing. Feeling the panic rising inside, Lizzie took some deep, slow breaths. In through the mouth, out through the nose. In through the mouth, out through—

'Are you okay?' Tim Faversham dropped into the seat beside her, studying her with concern.

'I'm good. Thanks.'

Tim was okay. He was unthreatening, and didn't push anything. As well, he'd proved an excellent dancer when he'd challenged her to try him out, the first day they'd met. Nor, in subsequent rehearsals, had he ever looked fed-up with her performance, but had seemed happy and relaxed. He'd been there for her all the time, anticipating her every move.

He hadn't tried to come on to her yet, either, which was a big plus point in her book. Would she ever be able to have another relationship, or would Bruno's brooding presence forever come between her and another man?

Her hands fisted. It would be better if people stopped walking on eggshells around her. It would give her a chance to find herself again. The alternative—take a long time out from ballet—was an unbearable thought. Although—she hesitated—she'd always wanted to teach, to choreograph, to direct a ballet. It was a frequent and very foolish daydream that one day, she could set up her own ballet school and company. Ha! That was something which would forever remain a daydream, unless she won an enormous amount of money on the lottery.

But maybe one day soon, she could try these roles at MetroCapital? Once she'd proved she could dance without Bruno?

Accepting Lizzie's reassurance, even though she realised he knew it wasn't true, Tim sat forwards, his forearms on his thighs, peering round her at the avenue of beeches. 'Posh approach. Reminds me of some chateaux in France, only they're often lime trees or plane trees lining the drives.'

'I've been to a couple of chateaux. They were disappointing in a way. No furniture or paintings, like our stately homes and even some of our castles have.'

'Much got confiscated, stolen or given away in the revolution, so my maman told me. I think her family lost a lot,' Tim said laconically. 'Look! There's the hotel. It's not too big and looks rather peaceful, doesn't it, tucked away down here?'

They'd broken out of the trees and were completing the last short section of drive, finally coming to a stop on the beautifully raked gravel outside a large, double-door entrance, standing open in the warm afternoon. Someone knelt under the windows along the front of the house, weeding the abundantly flowering beds. When the engine stopped and the door whooshed quietly open, blissful silence rushed in with fresh air, and once Lizzie stepped out of the coach, all she could hear was a gentle wind touching the trees, and the cry of gulls. The air was warm and scented, a gift from the flowers being tended by the gardener. She smelled an undernote of roses and something else, something she couldn't quite pin down. Was it to do with the sea?

As if in slow motion, the gardener stood and turned to watch the disembarking dancers. Lizzie froze, her eyes slowly widening at the sight of the tall, muscled man with wind-blown hair the colour of newly-shelled chestnuts. His green eyes roved over the group, over her. Then he stopped, for a moment utterly still as his eyes moved back to mesh with hers, and all around her the sounds of wind and gulls and voices ceased, and people stood immobile.

It might have been a year since they last met, but Lizzie knew him instantly. It was the sad man. Of all the people in the entire world, it was the sad man! Here, in this tiny place.

But how? How could it be?

Like a flicked switch, life resumed, but those few seconds of stark recognition between them were a catalyst for something.

She knew he, too, had remembered her, the moment she'd seen his eyes abruptly swing back and lock on hers, widening in shock.

'Lizzie?'

It was Tim again, his brotherly concern piercing her disbelief that *he* was here… and *she* was here. She'd no idea how it had transpired, but it was maybe the best thing which had happened to her for a very long time. The memory of the reception in Mondorra played through her mind jerkily, like one of the old silent movies.

She'd looked over to him, standing in the shadows, and felt a tug, which in view of where she was and who she was with, had shocked her. Stealing quick glances at Bruno, she'd kept her face impassive, caught her partner's arm, introduced him to the king and queen and laughed lightly, brightly. Another glance at the solitary figure, and for a second time, she'd experienced that indescribable pull. Against all common sense, apprehension nearly choking her, she'd been driven by a need to speak to him, imprint herself on his mind, and had gone over and exchanged a few words. She could feel Bruno's smouldering eyes burning a hole in her back, and had been relieved their conversation was short. Turning away, she'd seen the frown on Bruno's face, which had made her stomach feel cold and her legs like over-cooked spaghetti.

Now, stepping to one side, away from the chattering crowd of dancers, she waited, knowing he would come to her. She was aware of Tim watching curiously, his glance flicking between her and the man by the flower bed, who, after a moment of hesitation, strode across the gravel and stood in front of her. He looked dazed and as taken aback as she was.

'You look happier now,' Lizzie said softly, as if it had only been a day or two since they'd last spoken, instead of a year, although she'd often thought of him. She swallowed hard, a slight tremor shaking her body from head to foot. She dared not lift a hand in case everyone would see. Not just Tim's, but now other curious eyes watched them, wondering who this was, how she knew him.

'I am. I have been working, first in France, and then here for the last six months, and it has done me much good.' His eyes searched her face, looked past her at the other dancers, before coming back to rest on her. 'You... I can't believe this. You looked so apprehensive that night, and your wrist... I've never forgotten you. Is your dancing partner here? Are you still with him?'

When he spoke, it was with stilted politeness, but Lizzie could see a pulse beating frantically in his neck, under his strong, square-cut jaw, and noticed his hands were fisted, one clenched round the handle of a trowel until his knuckles showed white. But what had a gardener been doing at the king's birthday reception last year in Mondorra? He'd not looked like a gardener then. His fine evening clothes, his good looks and upright bearing, had all set him apart from everyone else..

'I broke up with my partner when we got back to England. What you said made me finally decide to leave, and for that I thank you. He also messed up with his dancing and is no longer with the company. I've not seen him now for, oh, it must be about ten months.'

His eyebrows flew up and a faint smile crossed his stern features. 'Good. It is better so, for I think he was not an amiable person.'

Tactfully put, Lizzie thought. He was the only person who had seen the truth.

He looked towards the door of the hotel where a tall woman stood smiling at William, their dance master for this trip, shaking his hand, nodding her head and laughing in response to something he said.

'I should be working. I am sorry. Please…' He stopped, biting his lip, still looking from the lady in the doorway and back to her, his face worried. 'Please, if someone says anything about us talking and asks you how know me…' Uneasiness crept into his face.

'What do you want me to say?' Lizzie asked gently. Her hand, steadier now, reached out to touch his arm just as it had last year. There was a mystery here. It seemed he also had secrets, and she understood his worry only too well.

'Please don't mention meeting me in Mondorra,' he finally said, his voice low, sweat breaking out on his upper lip which he swiped away with his free hand.

Lizzie looked at his mouth and decided it was beautiful then immediately felt guilty and anxious. She flicked a glance over her shoulder, but only the coach driver was there, his back to them both as he wrestled with bags and cases. Bruno wasn't watching. Bruno was gone from her life.

The noise around her and the sad man, as she'd always called him, dwindled as the chattering flock of dancers moved into the hotel. Tim gave her a concerned glance over his shoulder just before he also disappeared into the shadowy doorway.

Only the lady remained, waiting for her. Lizzie withdrew her hand, losing the subtle buzz of feeling which filled her both times she'd touched him, sparking something deep inside which she'd forgotten she possessed.

'No,' she said to the mystery man. 'No, I won't. Maybe you can explain later?' She spoke over her shoulder as she moved away.

'I can walk on the beach this evening—at around eight?'

'That sounds an excellent idea.'

Dazed, he walked away from her and round the corner of the house as Lizzie approached the entrance.

Looking curious, the woman held out her hand. 'Hi. I'm Emily Delamere, and I'd like to welcome you to Haven House Hotel. I'm sure you get sick of being told, but I've seen you dance and loved it. Loved *you*—you're so talented. I'd recognise you anywhere.'

'Thank you. I never get sick of being told,' Lizzie said softly. 'I like to be reminded sometimes, that I can still make people happy.'

'You've been given a room in the hotel, of course. Some dancers are in our hostel section, but they have all their meals with the rest of you. There's no need to register individually. Your ballet master has done a group registration and provided us with a list of names. Let me show you to your room.'

Emily directed Lizzie into a beautiful hall, with a Victorian desk acting as reception, then led the way up the curving, shallow-stepped stairs. 'When I first saw the house,' she told Lizzie, her eyes shining, 'I fell in love with the stairs. I wondered how many people had walked up and down them, or maybe even run, sometimes. So many stories waiting in the shadows and now no-one will ever know.'

Murmuring a suitable response, Lizzie wondered if this would lead to a question about the sad man, or the mystery man, as he now seemed to be. Indeed mysterious, if a well-dressed, handsome stranger had somehow morphed from a palace in Mondorra to being a gardener in a small hotel in Wales.

The question finally came when Emily had shown her a delightful room, windows open to the breeze coming off the sea, which was clearly visible at the bottom of the lovely gardens. As well as the salted breeze, there was a delightful smell wafting from a blue and white porcelain bowl filled with lavender flowers, sitting on a window sill in the sun's warmth.

'Let us know if you need anything,' Emily said. 'Wander wherever you like in the gardens, even the kitchen garden, where we grow food for the hotel. If you walk down to the bottom, there's a gate onto the beach. The cottage down there is private and is occupied by our head gardener, Claire, and her partner, Daniel, who's just recently come back from America.'

Ah. Not a question, but a warning. Lizzie was shocked at the tearing disappointment which ripped through her. So he was called Daniel and was newly returned from his travels, and he had a partner. That would explain his unease and his warning not to mention where they'd met. Black misery descended, shrouding her heart with despair. She should have known nothing could go right for her.

'I noticed you seem to know Anton?'

Lizzie looked up. 'I'm sorry? I thought you said Daniel—?'

'You were talking to Anton, our other gardener? You seem to know him?'

Lizzie sucked in a deep breath, as if reaching the surface after nearly hitting the rocky depths of a pool of deep, icy water. 'Anton? The gardener? Yes. Um, yes. We do. Know each other, that is. I, um, met him in London a couple of times. He's a dance fan. He attended class. We allow the public in to watch. Yes, that's it. That's where we met.'

There. She'd done as he'd asked and not told the truth about their previous encounter. But why did it matter to him so much? Her eyes flared open. Was he a wanted man? Was it wise to meet him alone on a deserted beach? Her hand came up to her throat as she stared out of the window towards the sea.

Giving her a slightly questioning look, Emily smiled, murmured something about coincidence and it must be lovely for her to have another fan around, then quietly left.

Sinking onto the bed, Lizzie laced her trembling fingers together.

What should she do? Why had she agreed to go along with his plea and the suggestion they could meet? Biting her lips, Lizzie agonised about going to the beach that evening.

Oh, she was being silly. At no point, either last year or now, had she felt threatened by him. Just the opposite, in fact. He'd struck her as troubled, yes, but not an angry person. Not like Bruno.

She deliberately closed down her mind, refusing to think about Bruno in this lovely place. He was in the past. It was time to move on.

CHAPTER 5

ANTON WALKED into the greenhouse and found Claire, her face brimming with a lively happiness he'd never previously seen until a man had turned up a few days ago and moved into the Gardener's Cottage with her. He assumed it might be Jamie's father and although curious, until now he'd remained, as usual, a silent observer in the background.

'Anton, good afternoon.'

He bowed his head gravely. 'Good afternoon. It seems you're most happy. Where is Jamie today?'

His response was automatic, clawed out of years of hiding his feelings, always being externally urbane and perfect, but inside, today, he was a melange of emotion. Joy warred with dismay. Amazement clashed with disbelief. Hope battled fear. It was so impossible this had happened. His dancer. The one who'd seen his unhappiness the night of the reception. Seen it, despite being on edge herself. On edge and almost fearful, he'd thought at the time. How could it possibly be that she was here? Had remembered him?

And then he'd told her he'd be on the beach this evening and had as good as told her to meet him there, implying he'd explain, for he'd seen the puzzlement on her face when he'd asked her not to tell anyone where they'd met.

What the hell could he tell her?

Claire regarded him with amusement, not seeing his distraction. 'So tactful. I am indeed most happy and owe you an explanation, I think. Jamie is with Daniel. Daniel Morgan. He's an artist.' The words bubbled joyously. 'Daniel and I are going to live together. He's Jamie's father, but last year there was stuff he had to deal with, so he went away, and now he's back. All sorted now.'

'Congratulations. I'm pleased for you.' And slightly amused, too, as he saw in his mind's eye the large Daniel Morgan seascape which hung on his bedroom wall back home. An original, which was called *The Passing of the Thunderstorm*. It was a tumultuous, living, breathing picture of wind-whipped waves, rolling black clouds with a flicker of lightening underscoring them in gold and sulphur, and in the distance, a promise of calm and sun, and he adored it. He looked forward to meeting the man who had painted such a wonderful picture, and maybe discussing art… but he was in the role of a gardener and not his usual self. Ah, well, even gardeners knew about art these days, especially in the egalitarian United Kingdom, so maybe he'd get the chance.

'You can be pleased for yourself as well,' Claire said over her shoulder as she turned to the workbench behind her, which stood at one end of the large new greenhouse.

'Oh yes? Why is that?'

'Because we want a bigger house, and that means you'll be able to move into the cottage. After all, it has to have a gardener living there, to justify its name.'

'Oh, well.' Anton shrugged as he tucked a tomato plant behind its support. 'That could take months.'

And he might have left. In fact, he might have to go tonight. If Lizzie wouldn't go along with keeping his secret and told people where she'd met him, then some curious soul would no doubt search the internet. His name wouldn't help, but if they took his photo and did a reverse image search, it would soon get out he was Crown Prince Maximilian, and the press would be curious. He'd prefer to be gone before that happened. At the moment, his fate was in Lizzie's hands, and all he could do was wait until he'd spoken to her later. The thought of leaving made him feel regretful, because he was really enjoying the hard work and fresh, outdoor life, as well as being very happy here.

'Don't be too sure. There's a house we know of which is empty. It had a long-term tenant who died, and the owner wants to sell. Apparently, we can rent it while we buy, as long as we can put down a deposit, which we can. Daniel's got to sell his flat in London, and he reckons it'll go fast because it's one of these trendy Dockland ones which he bought as an investment when he sold his old house. A couple of months, maybe, and it'll be ours. But because of being able to rent it, we can move in soon.' Again, her words came tumbling out breathlessly.

Anton's expression likely betrayed his slight shock. 'So fast? This has all been decided in just a few days?'

Did love do that to you? Make you behave with such impetuosity? How wonderful it must be, to be so sure, to not worry if it was the right thing, if it would be approved of. Just... to do it.

'We know what we want,' Claire said, cutting twine, 'and we've waited long enough. Do you want the cottage?'

'Well, of course. I would very much enjoy living there and thank you.'

Claire shot him another glance, brimming with amusement and excitement. 'I still love the way you speak. But do you know, I don't think I know any more about you now than I did the day I took you on? You never talk about your homeland, family, anything like that.'

'You can bait your line, Claire, but I'll not bite.' If he let something slip, his hard-earned tranquillity would disintegrate and this beautiful corner of Wales would be overrun with the curiosity seekers and press. He could only blame himself for being bored and becoming a bit of a European playboy, too much in the news for all the wrong reasons.

He hefted a ripe tomato in his long-fingered hand, the smell of the plants and fruit earthy and pungent in the warmth of the greenhouse. 'We need to pick many of these tomatoes soon, and take them to the kitchen for Jeff. Maybe Jake would like some, too, for the café?'

'I'm sure he would.'

They worked in silence for a while, carefully picking the fruit and laying it in trugs, the smell almost overwhelming as the crop was disturbed by their gentle hands. As he worked, his mind spiralled round and round the near unbelievable fact that Lizzie Cassidy was in the hotel and knew she'd met him in Mondorra.

Finally, unable to contain his curiosity, he turned to Claire, his hands stilling in their task of picking the fruit. 'Why is the ballet company here?'

'Outreach, they call it. It's a smallish group of dancers, and they do a few performances, give talks and demonstrations, invite you to watch class, go into schools. I saw them once when I was teaching in Cheltenham. They base themselves as centrally as they can and stay for about two months, I think. They have an itinerary. I need to check where they're performing. I'd love to see them dance.'

'Can you let me know, too? I enjoy ballet.'

'You know, Anton, you're a man of surprises,' Claire said, looking at him curiously.

'I hardly see it as any surprise I should enjoy ballet, surely? *You* do.'

Shrugging, Claire turned to put a full trug on the bench. 'I don't know. Here you are, out in the wilds of Wales, working as a gardener, behaving like a gentleman, very polite, but always so reticent about who you are or where you come from—gosh, that sounds like something out of a romantic novel—and now I discover you like ballet. Here.' She thrust the trug at him instead of putting it down. 'Take these up to Jeff.

He might need them for dinner, although I'm sure he's already organised. Ask him what other veg he'd like for tomorrow while you're up there, and we'll see what we can do for him.'

As he reached the hotel, Anton glanced at the coach, feeling a mix of anxiety and happiness. Lizzie was now here in Solhaven and could place him in Mondorra, but otherwise he was delighted he'd come across her again. The two emotions weren't doing much for his peace of mind. Anxiety shadowing his eyes, he slipped into the kitchen where Jeff and his staff were preparing dinner.

'Anton! Just the man. And bearing tomatoes. Wonderful chap. I can make that mozzarella and tomato salad now for a starter. What else have you got for me for tomorrow, eh?'

Anton placed the trug on a side table. 'Oh, a few things. Some early carrots. Lettuce. New potatoes.' He watched as Jeff lifted the tomatoes out. 'It must be very busy for you, with the ballet company arriving here.'

'I'll take the lot, and thanks. Can you get them up to me early? Yeah, because they're all eating in the hotel, even though the lower ranks are sharing in the hostel family rooms, we're definitely busier than normal.'

Anton smiled. 'The lower ranks are the corps de ballet, and the others will be soloists or principals, depending who they've sent. For something like this, just soloists, I imagine.' Apart from Lizzie Cassidy. What quirk of fate had brought her here, where he thought he'd be completely safe and unrecognised by anyone? And yet… and yet… how utterly wonderful and amazing and marvellous. It would shock Jeff if he performed his own pirouette, but that's what he felt like.

'How come you know so much about it?' Jeff ran the tap over the tomatoes, now transferred to a large colander.

Shrugging, Anton picked up the empty trug and moved towards the door. 'I quite like ballet. And yes, I'll bring that other stuff up as early as possible tomorrow morning.'

Making his way back to the greenhouse, he relayed Jeff's request for fresh vegetables.,

His mind kept returning to the ballet company and to Lizzie Cassidy in particular, who was both a threat and a delight. It would be better if he stopped asking questions and kept his distance from the company, and especially from Lizzie. She could so easily give him away, link him to Mondorra, and expose him for who he was.

Yet she was someone who had danced on the edges of his mind for the last year. Someone he might already be half in love with. He wanted to find out if it was an ephemeral love born from a fleeting encounter and imagination, or if it would stand up to reality.

'Where will they hold their daily class?' he asked now.

'No idea. The public room at the town hall, maybe. School doesn't close for another couple of weeks, so they can't use their hall. But daily classes? I thought by the time they reached a company like this, they'd know what they're doing? And I thought they needed barres and mirrors?'

'Like a pianist, they need to practice every day to keep supple and strong. I think they can rig temporary barres, but maybe they will do without their mirrors.' Anton gave her an amused sideways glance.

Claire looked at him, a question in her eyes which, he suspected, if she voiced it, would be like Jeff's—how come he knew so much about ballet?

He needed to stay quiet.

Rubbing his hand over his chin, rough with a dark chestnut stubble which he only shaved once every few days, he thought he'd like a shower and a shave before meeting Lizzie. It had been hot today, and he'd been working hard. His tee shirt and jeans were grimed. He glanced at his watch. It was nearly five. There would be plenty of time to shower, eat, and get down to the beach. Had he said eight? His mind had been in such a turmoil, he could hardly remember, but thought that was the time he'd suggested.

Which brought him another dilemma. Eat in the restaurant as he normally did, or keep out of the way until he'd explained? Although explain what, he hadn't quite decided yet.

Not eat at all might be his best option, considering his stomach was a churning mass of apprehension, anticipation, and fear.

Mindlessly, he swept the greenhouse, checked the windows, and after Claire and gone, made sure both doors were closed. He collected a couple of spades from the vegetable garden and put those and the wheelbarrow neatly in place under the lean-to built against the old grey stone walls.

Dinner forgotten, Anton retreated to his room and drank black coffee, staring moodily across at the hotel, one shoulder leaning against the wall next to the window. Shaking his head, he dumped the mug in the sink and stripped off, tossing his used clothes into the linen basket.

He welcomed the hot shower and the shave. He almost wished he could don a suit and tie and retreat behind the formality which had surrounded him all his life, before deriding his cowardice. If every time he came across a problem he wanted to run for the protection of the palace and his cloak of royalty, he was failing in his beliefs. He must stand equal and not fight his battles with his advantages, or he was learning nothing from his departure from Mondorra. Leaving his country had been a last attempt to gain his father's acquiescence to modernisation. He wouldn't weaken his position by a return to the old ways when doubt shook him.

Finally, he was dressed in clean jeans and a fresh, white tee shirt. Glancing in the mirror, he hardly recognised himself with his tough, honed body and sun-weathered skin, so different to the pale and urbane prince. He'd become the gardener he pretended to be. He ran fingers through still-damp hair, and left his room, a cold pit in place of his stomach.

Was there any way Lizzie might have worked it out? He'd not bothered much with the newspapers and hadn't turned on the small television since he'd got here, so he'd no idea if there had been anything about his absence, maybe a plea from his papa to get in touch.

If that was the case, though, surely Lizzie would have said something earlier? All he'd seen on her face had been bewilderment. If she got curious and looked up Mondorra, then she might find something. Oh, fuck! Just for the moment, his worries overwhelmed his delight. He didn't want to go back with his tail between his legs simply because he'd been outed. He wanted his father to realise over the passing of time that he was determined about his desire to modernise. He wanted his father to accept it and ask for his return.

What, anyway, could he tell her? It was too much of a risk, until he knew her better, to place the knowledge of his status into her hands.

His steps were slow as he descended to the beach, and his shoulders were bowed down with worry.

CHAPTER 6

Lizzie surreptitiously pulled out her phone to check the time. The dancers were grouped together in the dining-room, chattering loudly, excited about the programme of events coming up over the next two months, and the feeling of being on holiday, although there would be daily class and quite a lot of rehearsing. Tomorrow morning, there would be a meeting at Solhaven town hall, where they would set up their barres and do some demonstrations and lessons.

But tonight, all Lizzie could think of was Anton, the man she'd last seen at the royal reception in Mondorra, dressed urbanely and devastatingly in evening clothes, with shadowed eyes and sad face. The man she'd been compelled to speak to, despite Bruno's glower. To find him here was confusing, especially as he'd begged her, hurriedly and under his breath, not to say where it was they'd met.

'Expecting a call?'

Lizzie jumped and smiled nervously at Tim, sitting to her left. 'No. No, I'm just checking the time.'

'Do you need to be somewhere?'

She could tell, even as he smiled, he was asking a serious question.

'I—no. Well, not really.'

He regarded her steadily for a few moments. 'Anything to do with your hurried conversation with that good-looking gardener who gave the impression he'd seen a somewhat unwelcome ghost?'

Lizzie gave a huff of laughter and rubbed her hand over her mouth. If Tim thought she was interested in the gardener, would he become possessive, like Bruno? Would it make him mess her around when they danced, like Bruno? And then would it become all her fault, *again*?

'You don't miss a thing, do you?'

And yet through her fear Tim might show his true colours, she felt a twinge of relief he'd seen their exchange and now, she could tell him of their meeting, so if she never came back—oh! How dramatic. Of course she would come back. She'd already decided Anton was no threat, just as she also knew something indefinable drew her to him, even though he was, so far, a completely unknown quantity. She just hoped, like a moth to a flame, she wouldn't get burned again.

'What's the plan?'

'I'm meeting him on the beach at eight.'

'How well do you know this guy, Liz?'

His voice was concerned, not angry, and she relaxed a little. After all, ever since they'd started their dancing partnership, she'd talked to plenty of the other guys in the company, and he'd shown no possessiveness. 'Not at all. We've met once, and it's something about our meeting he needs to talk about, but I don't know what the problem is yet.' Lizzie fiddled with her spoon, pushing the rest of her pudding round in the bowl. Her appetite had been poor this evening, her insides a mix of excitement and trepidation.

'So where *did* you meet?'

Lifting her eyes, she looked at him consideringly, then shook her head. 'He came to watch classes one day, is all. We were both surprised to see each other today.'

'Oh, come on. Even I've realised we often get people in watching class and usually they're just wallpaper. Something must have happened?'

She searched his face but could still see no irritation or jealously. He looked worried, his brows pulled down, and he caught his bottom lip with his teeth, still showing nothing but a genuine concern for her. For a moment, she put Anton out of her mind and felt a softening blossom inside. Maybe Tim could become a trusted partner after all. Nothing so far had led her to believe otherwise, and this worry about her simply cemented their bond of friendship.

'I… look, Tim, it's not up to me. He's worried about something, okay? Maybe when I understand what the problem is, I can tell you a bit more.'

'But how on earth do you know if it's safe to meet him alone? Maybe I better come, too?'

Standing, Lizzie gave a gentle smile. 'I doubt I'm in

any greater danger tonight than I've been for the last three years.'

Leaving Tim looking stunned, she set off to walk to the beach, her hands clenching and unclenching by her sides, reflecting her apprehension. But she was also eager, and this surprised her, for after what had happened with Bruno, she'd wondered if she'd ever feel interested in a relationship again.

He was there before her, sitting on a rock, one knee pulled up, leaning back on his hands. The sun caught the rich hues of his hair, sparking coppery glints, and highlighted his lean figure. Appearing to be in a world of his own, he continued gazing at the shifting blue and turquoise sea, and when Lizzie stopped about two feet distant from him, he never moved.

'Anton?'

Visibly jumping, he sat upright and jumped from the rock, turning towards her. 'My apologies. You startled me. I never heard your approach.' He gave a quick smile.

'I'm sorry. I didn't mean to make you jump. Is there room for two on your rock?'

Anton looked startled and glanced at his impromptu seat. 'I think so. But... maybe only just?'

He waited until she'd pushed herself up with her hands and settled down before joining her. Their thighs were close. Very close. She trembled slightly, and sat on her hands to prevent it showing, biting on her lower lip as a nervous excitement swirled through her body, and her heartbeat became more rapid.

'The sea is a good place to be when you are troubled,' Anton said softly, leaning back on his hands again.

'It is, yes.'

A peaceful silence fell between them for several moments until Anton sighed and turned his head to look at her. 'You will want to know about my strange behaviour up at the hotel.'

Lizzie nodded. 'Well, yes, except I can't see why it matters. The lady who owns the hotel asked how I knew you. She must have noticed us talking.'

Lizzie was finding it hard to breathe. After just a few moments of closeness, butterflies had replaced the coolness, and warmth pooled between her thighs. Ever since she'd seen him in the palace, she'd felt this weird pull. A pull she'd covered up with chatter and dramatic gestures of her hands, designed to prevent Bruno from guessing this man could be important to her, and even though nothing had happened between them that night, Anton's words had triggered her final decision to walk out.

Sitting peacefully on the rock, with the evening sun glinting off the gentle swell of the water, and the smell of his freshly-laundered cotton tee-shirt and something more—him, she decided—now she could find out what it was, this spark between them.

And if he felt it, too.

'Anton?'

'I'm sorry. I have been thinking about what I should say. You understand I'm fearful if I tell you certain things, you might let it out in chatter. It would probably not matter at all, but... oh, I don't know.' He tightened his lips, his fingers playing with a bit of seaweed firmly rooted next to him.

'Answer some questions for me?'

'If I can.' He looked at her warily.

'Have you done anything criminal?'

Giving a short laugh, he shook his head firmly. 'That, I have most definitely not done.'

'Okay. Then are you a spy?'

His laugh, this time, was louder and longer. 'Your imagination does you much credit, but no, nothing so glamorous. Let me put it this way—I had a job, but the man I worked for, it was my father, thought it best to leave things as they have been for many years and wasn't interested in trying anything new. So there was nothing for me to work on, and as I told you at the reception, I lacked a purpose in my life. Your words triggered a final revolt, and I left, you know, the following day.'

'That was rather precipitate?'

'Ah, no, not really. It was something I'd been considering, just for myself anyway, so I could find a job. I've spent many years trying to change things. I hoped by leaving not only to find some employment, which I knew would relieve my stress, but also to make him realise the changes are necessary.'

'You look better, so I suppose working has helped you?'

'Indeed it has. I've felt so much better, and of course, I have had much time to think. My father has my phone number and can talk to me at any time, and I have a friend who is close to both my parents, so I hear the news. She tells me he has gone rather quiet and has spent much time talking to members of the… board, which might be a good thing if they agree with what I want to do.' Anton sighed and fell silent again, rolling his shoulders absently as if dispelling his tension.

Lizzie sat in patient silence. She knew when he was ready, he'd tell her the rest.

He turned his head and gave her a lopsided grin. 'The trouble is, I'm the only person who knows enough about the… the company to carry it forward, so he needs me, even as he refuses to accept my ideas. He might try to persuade me to come back, so I don't want him to know where I am. I don't want to return until he realises I have something to offer. My greatest wish is for him to phone me and ask me to come back, to work by his side, you see.'

'But what if he never rings?'

'I don't know.' He ran his hands through his hair. 'I don't think it will come to that and I'm very relieved he is speaking with others because I think he might finally understand what the company needs.'

By the time he'd finished his long explanation, he looked troubled. For the third time, Lizzie laid a gentle hand on his arm, felt its warmth, felt a shiver run through her from scalp to toes. Instinctively, she trusted him. Instinctively, she wanted to offer support. 'A difficult situation, and your father must feel very sad.'

'Yes, he probably is. As I am, as well. It will have taken him some time to realise the implications of my departure. So now he might think, and be sorry I have gone… At least, I hope so,' he finished under his breath.

'And you're sure you're right in what you want to do?'

He looked at her, his eyes steady. 'Oh, yes. Absolutely, yes. The big question mark over everything is whether he relents and I ever go back at all. But if I don't, the company will most definitely cease to exist, and I'm not sure how I feel about that. I think… I think I do not want it to collapse, because it is my inheritance and I care for it. But it has to modernise to be successful. It *has* to.' He murmured the last to himself, sadly, his eyes turning once more to look at the sea.

The timeless sea, Lizzie realised, which soothed you, and allowed your mind to empty and then, all being well, the best way forward would present itself. She wanted this to happen for Anton… and also for her.

'So it's simply you're worried, if I mention Mondorra to anyone, somehow your boss might hear about it and find you?' She was puzzled by his concern she should keep silent about where they'd met.

'I know, I know. It seems an excessive request, but… will you trust me on this, and *not* mention Mondorra?'

Raising her eyebrows, Lizzie gave a small smile. 'I will. And if anyone asks you how we know each other, I've already told the owner, and my new dance partner, Tim, we'd met when you came to watch class in London. Both of them had noticed us talking and asked.'

'Emily is very sensible. She'll drop it now.'

'You must remember, this is your family, Anton. Family is precious.'

'I know. I have spoken to my mother several times. I know she is sad, and I also know she is trying to fight my corner, for which I am grateful. But I don't want to be the cause of anger between my parents. I never want that.'

'Do they have a strong relationship?'

'Yes,' he said slowly, 'Yes, they do'

'Then that's good. I'm sure she knows exactly how to manage him.'

He gave her another sideways look and a lopsided smile, revealing the dimple in his cheek. 'Does your mama manage your father?'

'I don't know. I was brought up by my sister Christina. My parents were killed when I was young. I don't really remember much about them.'

'I am so sorry!' Anton's voice was shocked. 'That is very sad for you.'

'Yes, in one way. But Christina stands in lieu for me. She's sister and mother rolled into one. And now she's married to Dominic, and he's given me advice, too, when I've needed any.'

'Still, I'm sorry.'

They sat in silence for a few moments, both of them watching the endless ebb and flow of the sea.

'Come.' Anton jumped down from the rock and held out his arms.

It seemed completely natural to jump into them. Anton steadied her, and they stood, bodies touching, but not in an embrace. His hands dropped from her waist, then one moved up to cup her cheek. 'So beautiful. So fragile. Since I first saw you dance, you've been in my thoughts. When we spoke at the reception, you took up residence in my heart. I have been cross with myself that I just turned and walked away. Now I have found you again. I'm glad.'

Simple words, but poetic. Lizzie's heart, which had slowed its beat, raced again as he traced over her cheek, along her jaw, and let his hand drift gently to the back of her neck. One little tug. That would be all that was needed. One little tug, and their mouths would meet. Her eyes closed. There was a moment's hesitation from him, then the tug came.

Softly, sweetly, unthreateningly, their mouths touched. Touched again. Opened and flowered as she felt the hesitant caress of his tongue.

Their only background was the hushing of the sea and the cries of the seagulls. The beach was deserted.

She felt Anton release his gentle hold on her nape and slide his hands down her arms, seeking and finding her hands, winding his fingers in hers before stepping back.

'Lizzie.'

Maybe her name on his lips was only a whisper, a breath of air which floated off into the sky, but it brought her comfort. The depth of feeling he put into that one simple word was great indeed. It reached inside to her very heart and branded her with his caring. The gentle firmness of his clasp round her fingers reassured her. For the first time in many months, she felt her tension dissipate. She felt hope. And it was amazing, liberating, stunning, to feel it happen. Like a re-birth, back to a time when she would laugh and dance with anyone who was there, and speak without worrying about her choice of words.

Was healing that easy? Maybe… maybe.

Tears pooled in her eyes as she continued examining Anton's face, and his fingers tightened round hers.

'Lizzie?'

'I'm all right. I'm okay. Truly I am.'

'I must know—have I upset you with my kiss?'

'*No.*'

'I didn't mean to do that. Just, somehow, finding you again is a miracle for me. I'd walked away and left you at the reception, but I have wondered since if you needed my help. It was probably idiotic to think that because you were with all your friends. But… if it is not my kiss, why do you cry now?'

Lizzie dropped her hands and walked a little way, turning towards the sea. Her voice, when she spoke, was muffled. 'There are things inside me I need to get rid of. Things which hurt, but I'm finding them hard to talk about. I haven't felt happy for a long time, but just now, I saw my way back. I remembered how things used to be, before the last year or two, and I felt hope. That's all. That's why.'

He stepped up behind her and laid his hands on her shoulders, for a moment making her flinch until she realised this was still Anton. Maybe he was a completely unknown person with secrets of his own, but he was someone she connected with, and felt she could learn to trust. His breath was a whisper in her ear as he bent and kissed her neck where it curved into her shoulder.

'When you are ready, my Lizzie. When you are ready, if you want to tell me, I will listen.'

CHAPTER 7

Lizzie. Anton stood, still resting his hands on her shoulder, his chin on the top of her head. She leaned back into him, and the feel of her bottom against him, the smell of her hair in his nostrils, the memory of the sweet kiss lingering between them aroused him. He'd like to do more than kiss her, of course he would, but instinctively he knew Lizzie was fragile and needed care. He'd noticed her fingers relaxing within his, seen her shoulders droop and her look of surprise after their embrace. Then the tears had arrived, and panic had filled him.

What was hidden inside her? He suspected it had a lot to do with the bruises he recalled seeing on her arm and her ex, Bruno Bianchi, but she must decide when to talk. He wouldn't push things. His mouth curled into an ironic half-smile. It was odd. They both had something they were hiding.

Oh, sweet heaven, he really couldn't stay here with her pressed against him like this. His erection was hard and hot and this was so not the right time. Especially as she was standing still, almost as if she knew—well, she probably did! Surely, she could feel his response to her proximity?

Gently, he stepped back and kept a furtive eye on her as he readjusted his jeans, easing the pressure and lessening the visual indications. Drawing in a deep breath, thankful she'd remained standing with her back to him, he moved to her side and caught hold of her hand again. 'Come. I shall see you safely back to the hotel.'

'But won't it take you out of your way? I don't know where you're living?'

'I have a room over the garage, but soon I'll be living there, see?' He tugged her hand so she could see the small cottage he pointed toward. He could contemplate moving in as a distinct possibility and yet... perhaps not, if his father made contact. 'It's called Gardener's Cottage and is part of the hotel. Claire is the head gardener, and she has lived there for a year but now is to move into a bigger house with her partner, who is an artist.'

They walked back towards the gate that led into the hotel grounds, Lizzie looking curiously at the small house as they passed.

'Was it built for the gardener originally?' she wondered, her voice dreamy. 'Lucky gardener, if so.'

'I think, yes, it must have been. I had wondered if it was originally Garden Cottage, but no. The Victorian plans say otherwise, so I think it was for the gardener.'

'Victorian plans? This sounds interesting.'

'Emily and Claire want to restore the gardens as they were when the house was built. It's going to be an endless job.' He stared over the lawns rising to the hotel. 'A very long job, but they know what to do because the plans were with the house deeds and are dated. The cottage is a lovely little place. Very peaceful, and just look at that view.' Turning, he swept his arm in an arc, encompassing the sea, the beach, the sun gradually lowering towards the horizon.

'Do you think Claire will have seen us on the beach?'

'I think she might have gone with Daniel to look at their new house. They can rent it until they've completed their purchase, so maybe I shall move in soon.'

'Oh! If I'm not doing anything, would you like some help? I could clean. I'm quite good at cleaning.'

Anton detected a slight note of bitterness in her voice and felt sad. 'I don't need you to clean for me. Annie will send some of the housekeeping staff down when Claire moves out.'

'Who's Annie?'

'She is the mother of Jake and Claire. She is a kind lady. Jake and Emily own the hotel.'

'Family affair,' Lizzie said absently.

Anton noticed the figure of a man idly wandering in the rose garden below the terrace, stopping every now and again to bend and sniff at a bloom, gently caressing the petals. 'Your partner,' Anton said, his gut tightening as he felt a shaft of jealousy streak through him. 'He is more to you, maybe? As Bruno was?'

Surely not? Not after that kiss? If he was, Anton had

bitterly misjudged her. However, her next words lightened his expression and eased his mind.

'My dance partner only.' Her fingers tightened reassuringly round his. 'But he was worried I was coming alone to meet you, and I suspect he's been hanging around to make sure I get home safely. He's very sweet and kind.'

Anton nodded. Not like Bruno Bianchi, then, if he was a gentle person. One thing he was sure of, without Lizzie needing to tell him, was that Bruno had not been kind. The glimmer of fear he thought he'd seen on her face when she'd approached him at the palace had given it away, and the bruises had confirmed it. He'd been glad this afternoon, when Lizzie had told him she was no longer with Bruno.

'I will hand you over safely.' He dropped her hand and faced her, giving a slight bow. 'I must thank you for your discretion regarding Mondorra, but would you mind very much if this is not the end of our acquaintance? Would you perhaps come out with me one day, when you are not dancing somewhere? Maybe you are free next Sunday and we could go for a walk along the cliffs from the hotel? The views are incredible, and we can go as far as the headland.'

'I'd like that, and thank you. Where will I find you?'

'I will come for you in the hotel. Perhaps lunchtime? We can walk afterwards.'

'I'd like that,' she said again, smiling.

'I tell you another excellent place we could go is Silver Sands, where we could walk on the beach and eat at the café. The café does the most excellent food, I promise. But that would be more fun in the evening, to have our dinner then a walk, this time on the beach at sunset?'

'I read about the café online. Yes, I'd like to do that as well. Thank you.'

'Then we shall leave it there and plan for Silver Sands when I see you on Sunday.'

When she smiled and nodded her head, a rush of delighted pleasure and sheer elation spread through him. He would see her again. He would hold her hand again. Maybe they might even kiss again?

Glancing up, he saw her partner approaching, hands in his jeans' pockets.

'You will not tell your partner? Please?' Anton asked in a hurried whisper.

'I won't. Remember, we met when you came to watch me in a class. Hi Tim. Meet Anton.'

'Anton Monsarrat.' He gave another slight bow.

'Tim Faversham.'

The dancer held out his hand and the two men shook, Anton very aware of Tim's scrutiny. 'I am happy to meet you.'

'You're not from England.'

It was a statement, not a question. One of Anton's eyebrows rose as his head tipped slightly to one side. 'No. I am not. Europe is where I come from.'

'I'm from France. But my father's British so I'm bilingual. You also had the same good fortune, maybe?'

'I was taught to speak English, yes, from a very early age. But not every day. I am fluent but sometimes not so good with the everyday phrasing.'

'You know,' Tim said slowly, 'you look familiar, but I can't think where I might have encountered you.'

'I'm sorry, but I don't know you at all. I cannot see any reason we might have met. I am not from France.' Mondorra was bordered by France on three sides. If this Tim lived near Mondorra, it was possible he might have entered his principality and, at some point, seen him. And if Tim remembered, then he was another person Anton would need to beg for discretion. Hell! This whole thing might unravel so easily. What bad luck that two people on the same day should threaten his hideaway and therefore the occupation he'd grown to truly enjoy. It was a good place to be while he waited to hear from his father. He was never bored. The intricacies of the work on the Victorian restoration were enough in themselves to involve him, then there was the more general gardening work to be done. In this job, too, he was learning patience, for it took time for plants to reach maturity. He also had to listen to others, consider their plans, accede, fit in—he hoped all of it would stand him in good stead when he worked with the declining industries of Mondorra.

Tim Faversham stared at Anton, his head on one side, eyes narrowed, obviously determined to work out where they might have crossed paths.

'Do you not think,' Anton said with impatience, half turning away, 'it is simply you've seen someone who looks a bit like me and superimposed his features onto mine? I understand it can often happen like that.' He looked back the way he and Lizzie had come. The sun cast a fiery path across the waves. He folded his arms across his chest to prevent them trembling and wished this damned dancer would stop staring at him.

It was Lizzie who saved him. Lizzie, who maybe sensed his discomfort, and looped her arm through Tim's, turning him towards the hotel. 'Come, Tim. It's probably as Anton said. You've simply seen someone like him. I didn't eat much dinner. Let's see if we can find some supper. Maybe some hot chocolate and biscuits.' Over her shoulder, she smiled at Anton. 'I'll see you on Sunday for that walk you've promised me. I'll look forward to it. And your idea for an evening out? I can let you know a good day once we get our full itinerary tomorrow.'

'Can you also let me know where and when your company will perform? I would very much like to see you dance. Goodnight, Lizzie, and thank you.'

Anton stood and watched them walk away, shoving his hands in his pockets, looking troubled. He hoped Tim Faversham lived a long way from Mondorra and it was simply as he'd suggested—he resembled someone the young man had seen somewhere before. Although Anton had a distinctive look. And the European papers had loved to feature him in recent years. His shoulders dropped. Too much tension today, and it was telling on him. He was tired.

Tim and Lizzie entered the hotel, and as Anton walked towards the terrace, his mobile rang. Pulling it from his pocket, Anton glanced at the screen. It could be only one of two people—Beatrix or his mother—because his father had not, as yet, deigned to speak to him. A pity. He missed his papa, but he was always careful to send his love.

Beatrix.

'Hi, Beatrix. How are you?'

Anton diverted into the rose garden and sat on one of the benches. The roses reminded him of Lizzie—fragile and beautiful, but with a toughness underneath. As he listened to Beatrix, he frowned, and compressed his lips, replying in fluent French, which was the dominant language of his country. 'I'm sorry about my mama feeling so sad, but she must ring me. She could ring more often, I always tell her that, and she has this number, as you know. As for Papa, he understands what to do. He must acknowledge the fact that some of my ideas are worth putting in place.'

There was another outpouring from Beatrix. Anton jumped to his feet, feeling decidedly cross as his evening was ruined. The gentle warmth which had filled him while he'd talked with Lizzie was trampled under feelings of guilt about his parents—guilt which he fought, for what he'd done was necessary.

'I don't believe he's feeling unwell. I think it's just a ploy to get me to come home and then the same merry-go-round will start again. And also you told me he's been speaking to the Council, and you think it's about things I've suggested. So, no, Beatrix. Pleading on his behalf will do no good. When I left, I told my papa I wouldn't return until he realised the monarchy—the entire country—needs modernising. Until he agrees and asks me himself to come home, I shall stay for a while longer.

From what you've said, I think the shoots are coming up from the ground I prepared before I left.' He grinned wryly as the gardening terms slipped off his tongue.

Slowly, Anton sank back onto the bench, still listening. It was unfair of his papa to use Beatrix as an intermediary. He intended to text his mama and tell her it had to stop, especially as he and Beatrix were in absolute accord about not wanting to marry. Thankfully, her message delivered, Beatrix had moved on to the second women's refuge she was helping to organise in St Prasse, which sounded as if it was going from strength to strength. 'Well done, Bea. And yes, thanks, I'm well. Oh, listen to this. Do you remember my father's birthday reception last year and going to see Swan Lake? The same company have sent an outreach group to stay here, at the hotel, and Lizzie Cassidy is with them. She was the one who danced the lead. I must tell you—I have to tell someone and you're the only person I can at present trust—but I hope something will come of this. I've asked her to go for a walk with me, so we can get to know each other, but there's definitely something between us, and not just on my side, either... Yes, I know it will prove another cause for argument and dissention, for I'm sure my papa will deem her entirely unsuitable as the future queen of Mondorra. I haven't told her who I am, of course I haven't, but she recognised me from last year... No, she didn't know who I was then, either.'

After some more conversation with Beatrix, sympathetic to his dilemma about his parents and role in Mondorra, and his interest in Lizzie, the call ended.

For some time, Anton remained in the rose garden, a muscle in his jaw tensing, his hands occasionally fisting as he dealt with sadness and regret regarding his family, mixed with trepidation about Lizzie.

He'd told Bea he wanted to marry someone he loved. It would make the entire process of caring for his country so much more bearable if there was someone by his side in whom he could confide, discuss, play with, make love with, laugh with. He knew his parents loved each other, even though theirs had been an arranged match between two suitable minor European royalties. If only he could love Bea it would make things so much easier. As her father and his were such close friends, and she was considered a suitable rank, they'd been pushed together from being children. She was used to the pomp and formality of palace life. But love, sexual love, was sadly absent, and both of them were modern enough to reject coercion into marriage just because it appeared suitable.

He could imagine sharing his life with Lizzie, though. If she'd have him. He'd have to let her know his position before any mention of marriage was made, and although the allure of royalty attracted some women, he thought she'd be more the type to reject it. Reject him.

They were both attracted, that much he knew, but was this just casual for her? He didn't know her well enough yet to decide, and was very afraid he was already well on the way to being in love with her.

CHAPTER 8

THE OUTREACH GROUP spent their first few days doing daily classes and rehearsing for the demonstrations and performances they were planning on giving. It also gave Lizzie a chance to teach and direct the less experienced dancer in the group.

This was the first time many were performing in public and they were shaky and unsure. Lizzie worked hard to demonstrate correct positioning and how to present well to an audience. The younger members of the troupe, initially in awe of her, because of her standing, began to relax and ask questions. Lizzie spent more and more time working with them as William stepped back, obviously happy for her to instruct. Tim, William and she also discussed choreography, some of which needed changing for the small venues they would perform at.

For Lizzie, this proved a satisfying time. She enjoyed instructing and found the choreography something she had a lot of ideas for. She enjoyed working with Tim, too, who with his broader dance experience, could often suggest something slightly off-beat and quirky. Her earlier thoughts, as they'd arrived at Haven House, about teaching and maybe getting involved with the choreography, gained substance and she relaxed a little more. There was always, at the back of her mind, the thought she might never regain her previous abilities as a dancer, and even if she did, she only had a few years left in principal roles. This opportunity to teach and discuss what the group was going to do in certain dances showed her she had a flair, a knack.. This was something she was good at and had no connection to her past.

Their repertoire was repetitive, but it saved needing a lot of props, costumes and rehearsing. Lizzie was looking forward to the following week, when they'd start their visits, and was feeling more confident about dancing with Tim as each day passed. There was little to worry about here, in this informal and friendly atmosphere, working well with a group of inexperienced dancers and bringing out their talents.

As Sunday approached, Lizzie felt both excited and nervous. She'd not dated anyone for a long time, not since she and Bruno had first danced together. Even back then, they'd considered themselves an item, a partnership in love and dance, although the physical side of the relationship hadn't started until she was nineteen, and they'd not moved in together until she was twenty-six.

How quickly things had changed, she thought sadly as she ran down the stairs with the beautiful balustrade that Emily had raved about when she'd showed Lizzie to her room. But it was all gone. In the past, just as the stories of the people who'd lived here were in the past. Hopefully she would never encounter Bruno again, and maybe she and Anton would find they had things in common which they could enjoy doing together. She thought he was trustworthy, but his story about the business he worked for was a little strange. He'd told her so much but not really made anything very clear. No company name. No mention of what they did. So despite her inner attraction, she would stand back a little, observe him, use today to get to know him.

Standing in the doorway, Lizzie scanned the room. It wasn't hard to spot Anton—his hair was burnished in the sunlight streaming through the large windows. He sat with another two people. Who were they? She crossed the room toward them, feeling suddenly shy.

When she reached the table, Anton stood, a smile in his eyes, and took her hand, almost bowing over it. Her heart fluttered. Was he going to kiss it? But he let it go and pulled out a chair for her.

'Lizzie, this is Claire Bradstock, and her partner, Daniel Morgan. You should realise Claire is the main gardener here, and she is my boss.' He gave a gently self-mocking smile. 'Daniel is a seascape artist and someone who sells his paintings before he has died.'

Daniel let out a shout of laughter. He was a good-looking man with a strongly rugged face and dark hair. 'I suppose there's that,' he said. 'I think nowadays it doesn't apply much, though. Not like the past.'

'No,' Anton agreed. 'No, I don't think it does. I know

of several people who have bought paintings by people who are very much alive. I've seen an exhibition of yours, and I am glad to meet you so I can tell you how much I admire your work.'

'Thanks.' Daniel's comment was made by someone very confident of his own abilities, and yet it was also somehow modest. 'Lizzie, Anton hasn't told us anything about you, other than he was waiting for you when we hijacked his table. It's so incredibly busy today.' He looked round the room.

Indeed, every table was taken, and there was more staff than Lizzie had ever seen before, many of them youngsters being given the chance to earn some pocket money.

'I dance,' Lizzie said. 'I'm here with the outreach group.'

'Lizzie?' Daniel straightened, his eyes widening. 'Lizzie *Cassidy*?'

'Yes.'

'Anton never told us your last name. I'm quite a fan of yours,' Daniel said. 'Oh, my goodness, I last saw you dance about two years ago in Firebird and you were stunning.'

'He's not the only admirer of yours.' Claire leaned forwards. 'I saw you dance once, too. I was visiting a friend in London and she got tickets, but they were way up in the gods. I know Anton is keen to see a performance, and I think you can also count on Daniel and me in your fan club.'

Anton poured water for everyone and Lizzie took a sip.

'Is Bruno Bianchi here as well?' Daniel asked, looking round.

Despite the chatter and clinking of cutlery, a pool of silence fell on the table.

Daniel and Claire looked at each other, and Claire gave a slight shrug in response to his raised eyebrows.

Anton opened his mouth to speak, but Lizzie laid her hand on his arm and gave a small shake of her head. 'No, he no longer dances.'

Her voice was terse, and obviously sensing it was a sensitive topic, Claire and Daniel suddenly found the insides of their water glasses fascinating.

'Look,' Lizzie said, a tinge of sorrow in her voice, 'please don't feel guilty for mentioning him. Our names have been linked for so long it was hardly surprising you should ask. Bruno is ill and can no longer dance, that's all.'

Lizzie felt it was kinder to say that about her erstwhile partner. After all, he *was* ill. Addiction like his was definitely a serious problem.

'That's a hell of a shame—' Daniel began to say, but this time Anton spoke, cutting right across him, his voice smoothly urbane.

'Are you a fan of painting, too, Lizzie?'

She shot him a grateful look even as she noticed Daniel's surprise at the abrupt change of subject. 'Yes I am. I like landscapes and seascapes better than portraits. I've also seen some of your work.' She smiled warmly at Daniel. 'It was in a gallery I once visited in London. I liked it. There was one piece I fell in love with, called something like *Thunderstorm Passing* and was of wild waves and dark clouds, but there was a hint of the calm and sun to follow. No lightening but a yellow flare on the undersides of the clouds in one place. I loved it—could have looked at it for ever, I think. Way beyond my budget, I'm afraid.'

'*The Passing of the Thunderstorm*,' Anton said absently as he helped himself to water. Everyone looked at him, surprise on their faces. 'What? What is it I have said?'

'You know the painting?'

'I liked it too.'

But... how amazing Lizzie had liked it as well.

'Then... we must both have seen it in the same gallery? How strange.'

Anton smiled. 'Not so strange. Life can be like that. Times when perhaps you almost meet and it never happens until the right moment.'

'I wonder, though, what might have happened if we'd met then?'

'Probably nothing. It was a few years ago, and you would have been occupied with your dancing.'

And your dancing partner.

It was left unsaid, but Lizzie knew. Time to move on and leave Bruno in the past. She picked up the menu.

The server turned up, and they all gave their orders. Daniel offered wine, but Lizzie refused. She'd stopped drinking months ago in the vain hope it would help Bruno, and even now she saw little point in ever drinking alcohol again. It held too many painful memories.

Their chatter continued throughout the delicious lunch, touching on books, music, ballets, and painting, and ending up with Claire and Anton enthusing about the restoration project underway at the hotel. Lizzie was pleased to see Anton had only accepted half a glass of wine, and most of that was left at the end of the meal. She'd found his conversation informed and interesting. They shared an interest in many things.

Most of the diners had gone by the time the group stood.

'Would you two like coffee with us down at the cottage? I need to collect Jamie from Emily, then we're heading back. Jamie is our son.' Claire must have seen Lizzie's questioning look. She shot a look of adoration at Daniel, where it was mirrored on his own face.

The exchange made Lizzie feel wistful. Once, she'd thought she and Bruno had a love like theirs but it vanished, leaving nothing but sadness and regrets. Would she ever feel that way again? Even if she did, how would she know if it was real? She glanced sideways at Anton, who was explaining their plans to walk along the cliff path as far as the headland. Something indefinable pulled her towards this man and she thought he was someone she could trust. She'd enjoyed his kiss, too, and wanted to spend more time with him, but she was as yet uncertain what it would turn into.

Waving their goodbyes, they set off hand in hand, wandering through the grounds towards the gate onto the coast path. Anton explained the path dropped off the cliffs and ran along the beach at this point. If the weather was terrible, or the tides extra high, there was a diversion behind the hotel.

'You sound as if you know the area well. You've obviously put your spare time to good use?'

'I like to be on the go, I think is what you say? I've sat around for too many years feeling useless, and it's good to be employed with only small amounts of time off. You learn to value it and use it well. It's good, too, to work and be needed. It brings out the best of me, knowing I'm helping to feed people and to restore these lovely gardens.' His free hand encompassed their surroundings.

'Not so good on a winter's morning when it's cold and wet?'

'Ah, I've not experienced much of that yet. I came in January, when the mornings were getting a little lighter and the sun warmer. We've had rain, yes, but Claire leaves as much of the greenhouse work as she can, so if we have a rainy day we can spent some time catching up in there. It's good planning. We might get wet sometimes, but our skins, they are waterproof and clothes can dry. I like it.' He glanced down at her and laughed.

The cliff path wasn't easy. It wound up and down, following clefts inland for a while before heading back down to the cliff edge. Clumps of pink sea thrift tossed their heads in the strong breeze and the blue sea was flecked with white tops, while snowy gulls wheeled and turned, responding to their young whose squawking could be heard from somewhere out of sight on the face of the cliffs.

It seemed idyllic until Lizzie spotted something out to sea.

'Look!' She stopped abruptly and flung out her arm, pointing, a hand covering her mouth.

'Where? What have you—oh!'

They'd both seen it now. Three kayakers, quite a way out from shore. One had come out of his kayak and was clinging to the upside-down hull, but somehow, they'd got a rope attached so he was being towed by one of the others. They were making slow progress towards the cliffs and looked to be struggling.

Lizzie felt in her pocket and tightened her lips. 'I never brought my phone!'

'Neither did I. I wonder if they can make it as far as Haven Bay? It's quite a way for them and it means they'll have to turn sideways to the waves. That's not a great idea when the tops are showing white like that. It's a rough sea.'

'Oh, if only there was somewhere nearby where it's safe to land.' She looked to left and right, as if the solution would be apparent, but the cliffs were inhospitable and the waves crashed at the base, spray and water flying up a long way before spilling back into the heaving sea.

Anton hesitated then ran to the inlet at one side of them. To Lizzie it looked impossible to access, but after a few moments, Anton called over to her.

'Stay there. Beckon them in. There's a gravel inlet down at the bottom. I can just see it, and I think I can get down there. Once I'm down, they'll be able to see me and they will know where the inlet is. It will be impossible for them to see it otherwise. They have too much on their hands as it is.'

Hand to her mouth again, Lizzie watched as Anton disappeared down what seemed to her to be a vertical drop. Remembering what he'd said, she waved both arms, pulling them towards her repeatedly and let her breath out in relief as she detected a slight change in their direction so now they were heading straight towards her, and hopefully Anton.

Still gesturing, her heart was in her mouth, for she'd no idea if Anton had descended safely. It was quite amazing he'd given no thought to his own safety but had only shown concern for the people in the kayaks who were getting quite close. They changed direction again, their faces no longer looking in her direction, but towards the base of the cliffs, and her breath escaped in a rush. That surely must mean Anton was safe. They could see him. Her arms dropped. Now what could she do to help? What was Anton's plan? Surely he had one. He seemed calm and capable and had taken immediate control of something which could have ended up nastily.

Anton reappeared, making her jump. He had a rope in his hands. 'We're going to pull the kayaks up the cliff,' he explained breathlessly. 'They don't want to go any further. They're novices, now exhausted and cold. Haven Bay is too far, they have said. We have tied their rescue lines together to make this rope.'

One kayaker pulled himself over the edge and joined Anton, and both men hauled up the first of the three boats.

Lizzie heard the growl of engines as a lifeboat approached fast with spray from its bows fanning out on either side, smacking down onto the choppy waves with a clearly audible sound. Along the shoreline came the inshore rib, also scattering spray and bouncing about wildly, yet obviously well under control. Both wheeled round and idled, the lifeboat some way out, the inshore boat still within her sight, so not too close to the foot of the cliffs. There was more engine noise. She whirled. A coastguard Land Rover ground its way across the field behind, causing the cows to shuffle to one side, looking suspicious.

'Anton, see.' She pointed at the boats and then behind her.

He nodded tersely. 'Someone must have seen and called it in. No matter, they are safe now, and maybe the Land Rover can take them all back. They tell me they are camping near Solhaven.' He threw the rope over the edge, and it wasn't long before the second kayak appeared.

Within a few minutes, all three men and their kayaks were safe on the top of the cliffs. The coastguard got out of his vehicle and moved towards the shivering group.

Anton tugged Lizzie's hand. 'Come,' he murmured. 'My job is done. Let's walk on, before we get involved any further.'

'But shouldn't we stay and answer their questions?'

'There is no reason. The kayakers can explain. Come.' He tugged her hand and with one last backward look, they walked on along the path.

Much later, after an early dinner, Anton and Lizzie were sitting on the patio when Emily came out of the sitting-room, a uniformed man behind her.

Lizzie touched Anton on the arm. 'I think someone might be looking for you.'

Anton twisted his lips and glanced at the advancing pair, then at Emily, a glint of laughter in his eyes. 'I hope I'm not in trouble'

'Anton, I'm so sorry to break into your evening,' Emily said courteously, 'but Mr Williams has tracked you down by asking round in Solhaven for a "foreign chap who is a gardener", and he was directed to us. Something to do with a rescue?'

Mr Williams indicated a chair, and when Anton nodded and pushed it out from the table with his foot, he sat and cleared his throat. 'Are you the guy who sorted those kayakers out then?'

'I am.'

'Quick thinking. Lucky you didn't cause another casualty, though.'

'I knew what I was capable of,' Anton replied evenly, looking straight at the coastguard. 'If it had been too much for me, I would not have descended. No-one was coming to aid them when I made my decision.'

'Yes, well... you probably did some good. If they'd been thrown out, I admit we might have been too late. Anyway, you sloped off, see, and they wanted to say thank you.'

Anton raised an eyebrow, clearly confused by the coastguard's words..

'Left the scene, Anton,' Emily said with a small smile. 'But you're not in any trouble, or so I've been told.'

'Ah, thank you!' He smiled, then shrugged. 'I saw no reason to stay. I was taking Lizzie for a walk, the men were safe, you were there, and anyway, they had already given me their thanks.'

Looking from the coastguard to Anton, the frown back in place, it was clear Emily felt some concern for the hotel employee. 'What happened? Shall I stay?'

He looked at her in surprise. 'I don't mind whether you stay or leave. As you've just told me, I've done nothing wrong. There were some kayakers in trouble on the sea and one had already fallen out. I simply showed them where they could come in and land.'

'Climbed down the cliff he did, into Seal's Gully, see. Waved them in, then organised them to haul the kayaks up the cliff. The lads had told him they wanted to get out immediately, because otherwise they would've had to paddle over here, and they'd had enough. They were pretty shocked as well as wet and cold, by then.' Mr Williams folded his arms and sat back, nodding.

'Goodness. Why did they go out in such windy weather, with white caps on the waves?'

'Just what we asked them, see? Said they'd done a course here last year and bought the gear on that site which sells everything second hand and apparently it says you've "won" something if you pay the highest amount. Won. How silly is that?'

No-one supplied him with an answer.

'Anyway, down they come on holiday and as soon as they get set up, they're off in their kayaks. I'll be having words with that course organiser. He needs to make sure his pupils know which weather to avoid. Off-shore wind and white caps—lethal combination.'

Emily was becoming engrossed in the story, but

Anton was looking distant. Lizzie smiled as he folded his arms across his chest and leaned back, crossing his legs at the ankles as he prepared to wait it out.

Finally, the man got to the point of his visit. 'The lads you helped, they said they're going to sell the stuff as soon as they get home. But I'm curious—you seemed to know exactly what to do?'

This time, Anton gave a visible shrug and explained his reasoning. 'I know it can be very hard to find places safe enough to land, but if you're travelling along a coastline and back, it is wise to find a few. Then, if there are problems, you know there's somewhere you can go. Yesterday, it was too rough to be close to the base of the cliffs, and they are hard to spot if you have to stay further out. I was directly above one, so I asked Lizzie to wave them in, and when I could see them, I waved too. That's all.'

'But you climbed down into Seal's Gully, lad?'

Another shrug. 'I have done rock climbing as well. But it wasn't difficult, otherwise the men couldn't have come up after me.'

'Quite the action man, eh? Those men were scared witless by what had happened. Some steep rock slabs would have seemed nothing in comparison, I suppose. Anyway, they wanted me to give you this envelope, and asked if I'd thank you if I found you.'

, Anton opened it, one eyebrow raised. There was a note repeating their effusive thanks of earlier, and a chunk of money, which Anton didn't even bother to take out of the envelope. 'Kind of them. I will keep the letter, but the money can be given to the lifeboat. I know there is one in Solhaven.'

Mr Williams rose to his feet. 'Right, then. I'll be off. Well done, lad. Good work, and thanks for the donation.'

Lizzie was quite thoughtful later that night. Ready for bed, she stood gazing over the lawns towards the sea. Even though dusk had fallen, it was still blue. The liquid gold of the sun's reflection shimmered on the gently shifting water, much calmer now the wind had dropped.

If that had been Bruno on the cliff, he would have done nothing. Probably suggested walking on, calling them idiots, behaved in his usual self-centred and selfish manner, which had become his norm.

Anton's character was very much the opposite of Bruno's. He'd remained calm, had assessed the situation rapidly and found a practical solution which had undoubtedly saved lives. Nor had he even wanted to stay and play the hero, the bit Bruno would really have enjoyed and wallowed in. As for the money, Bruno would've grabbed that and bought himself a bottle of whisky and no doubt some cocaine, not immediately dismissed it and given it as a donation to a worthy cause. And thinking about it, Anton's wages couldn't be very great.

Anton's behaviour had made a hell of an impression on her all round. He struck her as a steadfast character who wouldn't shirk his duties lightly, and she hoped, for his sake, his father would see sense and invite him back to help move their company forwards.

Yet if he did, what then of her? Would it matter to her? Would she mind?

Leaving the curtains open, she sighed. Yes, it would matter, and she would mind. Damn it, she'd mind very much. She was intrigued by Anton, and very much wanted to get to know him better and as the day had passed, she felt more and more here was a man she could trust.

CHAPTER 9

SEVERAL DAYS PASSED in a blur of activities for Lizzie,. The outreach had begun and every morning after class, which was open to the public to watch, they'd driven off in their coach to various towns and large villages, where they'd done another morning class and sometimes given either an afternoon or an evening performance. Although schools were closed for the summer holidays, they'd known beforehand about the company coming and had organised for the children to come in on the day the ballet group was due to visit their town. Interest had been great, and two or three ballet schools had approached them to see if any of the group could come in to give a talk.

One morning, they set off for a town about twenty miles distant, passing through Solhaven, which was always a slow experience. Their coach was plain, with the logo of the hire company, so not identifiable as the MetroCapital group's transport, but by now many people in Solhaven recognised it and would wave as they passed. Lizzie was daydreaming, her head resting back against the seat, a small smile on her lips as she thought of Anton and his prompt actions last Sunday. Such decisive behaviour, with no dithering or wondering what should be done—just immediate action which had, if not saved lives, certainly had meant less fear and misery for the kayakers.

Being here was indeed doing her good, but not simply for the lack of pressure and holiday atmosphere. No, it was reconnecting with Anton which was having a profound effect on her. They'd snatched a few moments every day to sit and have a coffee and talk. He'd suggested she wasn't to go walking after such a long day and needed to rest. She adored his care of her, loved their conversations, and looked forward every day to the moment the coach drifted down the drive and halted by the hotel entrance. She immediately scanned the grounds, and if he wasn't in sight, she'd go to her room to change and shower, and then she always found him waiting on the terrace or in the sitting-room when she descended.

In his company she was relaxing more and more, opening up to him more and more. He was fun.

And sexy.

Oh, yes, sexy indeed, and she knew she was interested in more.

As they crept round the roundabout at the bottom of the high street, Lizzie glanced out and tensed. There had been someone in the throng of holiday makers... Her head twisted as she tried to look back, but the coach was finally free of the slow queue and picking up speed towards the open road.

She must be imagining it.

Her hand came up to her throat and her heart pounded, her eyes wide as she contemplated what she thought she'd just seen. Not what, though, but *who*.

Surely she had imagined it?

There was no way it could have been Bruno. It was like when Tim thought he knew Anton, and Anton had said he was probably remembering someone similar and mixing them up. Of course! After all, she'd only had a glimpse of this person, who might just have been a similar type. That was all. As they drove to their destination, her heart slowed. She sank back into her seat and convinced herself it had all been her imagination.

By the day's end, Lizzie was cross with herself. Tired and slightly dispirited, her thoughts had returned to the past while she danced a short pas de deux with Tim, and she'd hesitated and lost her step. Tim had been great and swirled her round in an un-choreographed pirouette and she'd regained her control, but she knew it all stemmed from thinking she'd seen Bruno in Solhaven. Ever since she'd left him, she'd erected a barrier and stashed all the bad stuff behind it. Anton and the outreach were giving her some self-esteem, but she knew she had to trust someone and let it all out soon, before it swamped her. The barrier was weakening and the pressure behind it would soon burst through. She wanted an end to the churning thoughts and self-blame which still haunted her, even though it was a year since she'd left Bruno. Biting on her lip, she stared out of the window, not seeing the beautiful countryside passing by outside.

'Hey,' Tim put his hand on her arm, immediately understanding her despondency. 'It wasn't that bad. I was the only one who picked up on it. Stop worrying. I don't know why you doubt yourself. You're a fabulous dancer, okay? It's probably my fault, because I know I'm not as good as Bruno.'

Not what Bruno had told her. Even before the drink and drugs had taken hold of him, he'd made joking comments about how she was only great because he'd chosen her as his partner. Looking back, she slowly understood it was Bruno who had always been on the edge of doubting himself, Bruno who had lacked confidence, and had bolstered himself by blaming her and using substances. But there was a long road to travel yet before she really convinced herself of that, before she could shed the feeling it was all her fault everything had gone so horribly wrong.

Lizzie glanced at Tim, a half-smile on her face. 'Ah, no, it's not because you're not Bruno. You're a brilliant partner—very kind, very forgiving, and immensely supportive. Thanks.'

It amused her to see him blush faintly, but by now they both knew any love interest was a non-starter. They liked each other and were becoming good friends, but anything else—any spark—simply wasn't there. Which, as far as Lizzie was concerned, was great. She spent altogether too much of her time dreaming about a tall, chestnut-haired gardener with troubled eyes and a sweet mouth. She was grateful she didn't have to fend Tim off as well.

Lizzie descended the steps of the coach and stood for a few moments with her eyes shut, hearing the distant sound of the sea and smelling the flowers. A few birds chirruped desultorily from the trees, but it was too early for the evening chorus and it seemed none of them had any interest in producing a proper song. Oh, yes, this place was well-named Haven House, and Dominic had been right. It was a peaceful place, and it gave her hope that one day she'd conquer everything—her fears, her moments of hesitation and lack of emotion—and could dance again upon the world stage.

'Lizzie?' Tim nudged her.

Opening her eyes, she saw him tip his head towards the side of the house. 'Anton's waiting for you.'

Glancing across, she took in his easy stance, the dark jeans showcasing long legs, and today, a green tee shirt which surely would reflect the colour of his eyes. Her cheeks flushed, and a frisson ran through her, one of secret delight at seeing him even though they'd sat late last night out on the terrace. She'd wondered if she'd ever feel attracted to, or trust, another man, but it seemed it was easier to do than make a full return to dance.

Standing still, she waited until the dancers had flocked inside, hungry as always and in search of their evening meal, then walked towards Anton, who by now was also moving towards her. They stopped with about a foot of space between them, and he slid his hands into his pockets, maybe to remove the temptation of touching her in full view of the hotel. She, too, had to resist stepping forwards, leaning into him, smelling the warm cotton and musky scent of him.

'Emily told me you where you were dancing this afternoon, and Claire let me leave early. It was not too far, and I had time to get there, so I took my car and came to watch. You were stunning, Lizzie.'

'You came to watch? Why not stop by afterwards to say hello?'

'I thought there was no need as I intended to see you later, and I thought you would be exhausted and maybe just wanted to rest on the journey back and not to entertain me.' He gave her his quick, warm smile.

There it was again, a sweet and considerate thought. The ice encasing her heart, which had already started to melt when she'd first arrived at the hotel, melted a little more, and instead, hope took seed.

'Thank you.' Her voice was subdued.

'Lizzie, you seem to be a little quiet tonight. Are you okay?'

She raised startled eyes and met concerned green ones, a slight frown creasing his forehead. 'Yes. I'm—no. No, I'm not okay. When we went through Solhaven this morning, I thought I saw Bruno, which is completely silly, but it spoiled my day a bit, and I made a mess of the afternoon performance. I'm surprised you didn't spot it. Tim was great and covered for me, but it was so stupid to let it bother me.'

'Is it likely Bruno would be here?'

She could see by his frown he was concerned.

'I don't know. No. There's no reason he should be.

He… he threatened me when he was fired by the company, but I've never seen him or heard from him while I was in London, so why would he come down here?'

'Unlikely, I agree.' Anton worried at his lower lip. 'Unlikely. But if you think you saw him, then maybe take a little care for a few days, just in case? Although I really think if he was going to do any harm, it would have been immediately after the company asked him to leave, when maybe he was in a temper.'

Lizzie pressed her lips together and nodded, feeling the wetness of tears in her eyes, which she blinked away furiously.

'Now look, if you are feeling sad, why don't we go to Silver Sands, to walk and to eat at the café? I assure you, the food is very good. It is Jake who cooks it, and he is the owner here as well. He and Emily.'

'Does he cook the food here as well?'

'No. Jake has told me he prefers to keep his café, and he leaves most of the hotel for Emily.'

After a moment of thought, Lizzie nodded. 'Give me fifteen minutes to have a shower and change?'

'I will bring my car here and wait. It is red.'

Within twenty minutes, dressed in white trousers and a lilac shirt, Lizzie had returned. An evening spent in the company of Anton was just what she needed, and she was grateful he'd noticed she was down-hearted.

It surprised her the rather luxurious car had foreign plates and a left-hand drive, and as she slipped into the passenger seat, she commented on it immediately.

'The car is French. People in Mondorra often have

cars registered in France because we border their country. I can drive perfectly well with the wheel on the left, but I don't overtake unless I am on the motorways. It was easier to come away with my car.'

With casual ease, he put the car into gear and they set off sedately up the drive to the road.

It took only ten minutes before he pulled into a car park, still very full, even though by now it was after seven in the evening. Despite the number of cars, the beach was large enough to absorb everyone. Admittedly, there were a few clusters of people with windbreaks and barbecues around the slatted walkway leading onto the sand, but after that, everyone was scattered.

Curious, Lizzie took in the breathtaking beach, backed by low cliffs and dissected by jutting ribs of honey-coloured rocks, with gently-rolling green hills and white-painted cottages behind. The sands were golden and the blue sea creamed gently onto the beach. She could smell seaweed and delicious food mingling on a gentle breeze. Children laughed and ran about, or sat digging castles with great concentration. In the sea were swimmers and further out, a few surfers. Turning, she saw the café with wetsuits and surf boards on racks outside, as well as net baskets haphazardly filled with buckets, spades, brightly-coloured balls and very necessary windbreaks. It was pure seaside, and she loved it. Spreading her arms wide, Lizzie gave a delighted smile and spun round in a graceful pirouette.

'I am pleased you like this place. Now, tell me—do you want to walk or eat?'

'Oh, eat. I'm starving.'

Anton caught hold of her hand, and they turned and walked over to the café, which had outside tables and good-sized indoor seating with large glass windows allowing a view towards the sea.

'In, or out?'

'If you don't mind, I'd prefer to go inside.'

Anton opened the door and ushered her through, and they stood for a moment before, as if of one mind, choosing a table over by the window, grinning at each other as they sat down.

A menu was brought to them, and as he took it, Anton spoke to the server, whose name badge declared her to be Angelina. 'Is Mr Jake Bradstock still here?'

'Yep, he is, although he muttered something about having to get off soon to give the baby her bath.' The girl smiled, obviously amused by this.

'Can you say to him Anton is here and would like to introduce Lizzie, who is a dancer.'

'Oh!' Angelina turned a wide-eyed gaze to Lizzie. 'Oh! I recognise you. I came to watch the class and then I saw you dance the other night. You're beautiful. I'd love to dance like you.'

'Thank you. Have you tried ballet?'

'Me? Huh! Can't see me galumphing round stage.'

'Ballet at any age is good for posture, the way you walk and carry yourself, even if you never take it further than some basic work. You should try it sometime. And you never know—you might end up being very good. You don't know until you try.'

Looking dazzled, the young girl smiled her thanks

and moved off. 'I'll get Jake. Would you give me your autograph before you leave?'

Whirling in a sudden attack of shyness, she disappeared through a door over by the cash desk and within minutes, Jake had appeared in her place.

Lizzie had met Sasha and Emily, but had not yet met Jake, who was Emily's partner, husband. She wasn't sure. His stunning good looks immediately struck her. His face was thin and intelligent, with deep blue eyes and a cloud of curling, sun-bleached hair falling to his shoulders, through which he was running his hands.

'Hi, Anton. Even after all these years, I still hate the hair nets. They give me an itchy head. How are you doing? Is Claire keeping you under control?'

'I am good, thank you.' Anton smiled and Lizzie caught her breath and shifted in her chair when he turned the smile in her direction, his eyes crinkling at the corners, a dimple appearing in his cheek. Jake was good-looking, but Anton was exceptional, as far as she was concerned. 'This is Lizzie Cassidy, Jake. She is one of the greatest dancers there has ever been. Lizzie, this is Jake, who owns the café and cooks many of the meals.'

At his words of praise, Lizzie felt her cheeks flush, and she gave a small shake of her head. 'Hello, Jake.'

'Hi. Are you enjoying your outreach so far?'

'Indeed I am. We all are. Your hotel is beautiful and so restful.'

After a few more words, Jake took himself off to give his daughter Olivia her nightly bath, a ritual he seemed to love. As he left, he jokingly commented he'd made a mini surf board to go in the bath, and she was already grasping hold of it and showing great promise.

'Nice man,' Lizzie commented when he'd left. 'What on earth was he on about, making a surf board? For a baby? How old is she, anyway?'

'She's seven months old. I forgot to tell you before, when I was talking of Jake, he was once a surfing world champion, and Claire has told me he wants to teach his daughter from a young age.'

'*Young*? Seven months? Oh, my!' Lizzie laughed aloud before clapping her hand over her mouth, looking round guiltily.

Anton gave her a concerned look, one of his brows flicking up, and he reached out his hand and took hold of her wrist, pulling her hand away from her mouth.

'Lizzie, Lizzie. There's nothing wrong with having a good laugh. It's allowed. It's natural. Especially about Jake teaching Olivia to surf in a bath! I think everything is tightly locked down with you.' His fingers were gentle, and as soon as she'd dropped her hand onto the table, he let it go, still looking at her with worry on his face.

Her laughter was still bubbling up, but somehow it got stuck in her throat and erupted from her in a sob, tears escaping from her eyes. Lizzie didn't know what to do and shot to her feet, her hand coming back up, this time to stifle her weeping. She looked wildly around, saw the astonishment of Angelina, who was approaching their table with her tablet in hand, presumably to take their order. A few of the other people in the café turned their heads, whispering, looking at her, and she knew it was because it was her fault, *it was her fault*. That's what Bruno had always told her—whenever anything went wrong, in a rehearsal, on stage, when they were socialising, talking to other men —it was always her fault.

Insides churning, she turned, and made a dash for the door, shooting through it at speed before running blindly across the car park and onto the beach. She kept running until she could hardly breathe, and still she cried. A slab of rock loomed in front of her and there she stopped and turned, leaning back against the warm stone, her eyes closed, the tears pouring down her cheeks.

She was a fool to have feelings for Anton. She didn't deserve to be happy. She'd reassured him she'd not mention Mondorra, and she should have ignored him after that, no matter how much she liked him. What if she had seen Bruno, and he was watching her and knew about Anton? Fear caused her nails to dig into her palms, and she shook with misery. He might hurt her. He might hurt Anton.

What would Anton think of her now? His swan princess had feet of clay.

CHAPTER 10

ANTON SAT STARING at the empty seat opposite, his foot tapping on the floor, fingers interlaced tightly. He was thinking about Lizzie's reaction. At the reception, back in Mondorra, he'd suspected Bruno was being abusive towards Lizzie. There had been those bruises on her arm, her apprehension, Bruno's glowering presence. This morning, she thought she'd seen him in Solhaven, and she'd clearly been frightened. It was most unlikely it had been Bruno, but the mere possibility would be enough to revive unpleasant memories, perhaps? This should have been a pleasant evening's trip to the beach, and when they first arrived, she'd seemed enjoy everything. The beach, some praise from the server, and a pleasant chat with Jake.

But then came her joyous laugh, which she'd tried to stifle.

Poor Lizzie.

And yet… it was possible her mind was ready to release its burdens.

Anton nodded at Angelina. 'We shall be back. Miss Cassidy has suffered a recent sorrow, and she occasionally feels very unhappy.' He stood and quietly left the café. Once outside, his movements became more purposeful as he strode to the edge of the car park, looking round anxiously. Where had she bolted to? Ah, there—leaning against a rock a little way down the beach. A great relief flooded him,

Unhurriedly, he walked towards her, giving her time to weep, and when he reached her, he leaned back on the rock himself, his shoulder touching hers, his hand loose, fingers brushing the back of her hand to show her he was there. Her sobs lessened. She looked so weary, traces of her tears marring the porcelain beauty of her skin. Anton's heart broke for her. She was carrying a very heavy burden, and he so wanted to help. The question was, would she share it? Without a doubt, Anton knew it would concern Bruno.

Finally, Lizzie fell quiet, apart from an occasional hiccup. Anton pulled a pristinely white handkerchief from his pocket and tucked it into the hand next to his. Her fingers clutched it convulsively before she slowly lifted it to her face and began the mopping up.

When she was still again, he finally spoke. 'Would it help to talk, do you think? I feel you have kept a lot bottled up inside and something has finally caused you to break down—maybe thinking you saw Bruno? Perhaps better to get rid of it all now?'

'I'm so sorry. I've spoiled things. This was supposed to be a pleasant evening out and I've spoiled it.'

The guilt and, again, that barely discernible thread

of fear, as if she expected him to react angrily, made his heart sore. 'Hush. You've spoiled nothing, hear me? The café is still there, and we can eat later. The sun is still shining. We are on a beautiful beach. You have spoiled nothing for me, but only for yourself, and for that, I am sorry.'

Lizzie heaved out a breath. 'Can we walk?'

'Are you sure you don't want to sit down for a short time and maybe have a cup of coffee and a piece of Jake's cake?'

Giving a small smile, she straightened up from the tilted rock slab and wiped her hands over her jeans. 'Not yet, but maybe later? Is that all right?'

Side by side, they meandered along the beach. Anton took her hand, a warmth spreading through him as her fingers tangled trustingly with his. He'd sometimes wondered if he could please his papa by marrying Beatrix, because after all, they were good friends, but after meeting Lizzie again, properly meeting her, he knew it would have been a mistake. His feelings for Lizzie were so very different—a mix of caring, lust, and friendship—and he wanted to look after her and keep her safe. Quite what she'd think of who he was, he'd no idea. For a brief, wild moment he wondered about never going back to Mondorra, staying here for ever in this enchanted small corner of Wales, gardening for the hotel, living with Lizzie in the cottage. But only for a moment, because he knew he could lead his country into a better future, given the chance. But would Lizzie want to be by his side? Ah, that was something to think about later. For now, he must focus on Lizzie and her pain.

After a few moments, his voice gentle, he asked the question which had been at the back of his mind for a long time. 'I think maybe Bruno is behind all this upset?'

'Yes.' Her voice was low as she slanted a sideways look at him. 'Because I thought I saw him today, it threw my dancing off kilter, and I've been thinking about him, about the last couple of years we spent together.'

'Off kilter? This is something new to me.' Anton gave her a small smile, hoping to cheer her up with his misunderstanding, and squeezed her hand.

'It means I didn't dance every well. My concentration wasn't fully on what I was doing.'

'I see. Do you want to tell me about Bruno and what happened before he left the company? I ask, because sometime when we let things stay inside us, they fester and cause harm. I know. For several years I have kept the feelings about my situation too close. When I eventually laid out my thoughts and my ultimatum, I felt much better because then we all knew what the truth was and how upset the situation had made me. It's hard to speak out sometimes, because we can hurt others if we do, but it is better in the end.'

'You're a wise person. Very sure of yourself, too. I used to be sure of myself, once.'

Anton pulled her gently to a stop and turned her to face him. He wrapped her in his arms and swayed gently, his cheek resting on her hair. 'I am not sure of myself at all,' he murmured, knowing what he said was true. 'I am still worried about my decision, even though I feel better, now the truth has come out between my parents and me. But you must feel ready to speak, too, and if it is now, I'll listen.'

'I love the way you speak.'

Anton pulled away and laughed. 'Surely, I speak like you? Yet Claire has also commented, and once, Jake said he knew I wasn't English because of the way I speak. Come on, now you must tell me! What is it I am doing wrong?'

Lizzie gave a watery smile, and they continued to walk along the beach, hand in hand. 'Your English is amazing. It's hard to pinpoint, but you're more formal. You don't shorten words—we call it contracting—like it is to "it's". Or we are to "we're". Well, sometimes you do, but not much. And sometimes your sentences can be phrased differently to the way we'd say something. That's all. Nothing to worry about.'

'I think when I was a student I spoke more easily because I was here for four years altogether, but it's twelve years ago now and in all that time, I've stayed in Europe.'

Should he just let the subject of Bruno and all her misery go? Yet he felt he'd be letting her down if he didn't get her to open up. He would ask her one more time.

'Do you want to talk, my Lizzie, or shall we now forget your tears?'

For a few moments, Lizzie remained silent. Anton looked sideways at her and saw her frown as she bit down on her lip. He wanted to help, but it should be her decision to talk to him.

'You must realise,' she said, abruptly breaking the silence, 'Bruno changed. When we first met, he was fun, and a fantastic dancer. We'd joined MetroCapital corps de ballet and the company pushed us to dance together. We were happy to oblige, and we knew we were good as a partnership.' Lizzie stared out across the sea, looking sad. She scrubbed the back of her free hand across her mouth before turning to look at Anton. 'We fell in love, too, although I sometimes wonder if that was just youth. The ballets we danced in where the principals were always in love, the fact we were so close as dance partners. It was almost expected of us, if you can understand.'

Anton raised his brows, shaking his head at the similarity to his own situation. Yes, he did indeed understand how easy it might be to take up with someone just because expectations were strong. He and Beatrix had needed strength to resist because of their easy friendship and similar backgrounds, so he could understand how Bruno and Lizzie had slipped into their relationship. 'Go on, my Lizzie.'

'It only went wrong about two years before they threw him out. Maybe we saw we weren't a great match, I don't know, but he had some affairs and flaunted them in my face. That I could cope with, but he got in with the wrong crowd and was drinking too much and taking drugs. He'd always used a bit, but this was much worse, and I didn't know what to do.' She clutched his hand so hard he winced. He pulled her into another hug, this time his hand smoothing up and down her back as inside he ached for her, felt her pain, wanted to wipe it all out.

Her voice was muffled as she continued to pour everything out, her face against his chest. 'It was no longer about whether we loved each other—this spilled over into safety when we were dancing, and I didn't know if I should tell the director. His character changed, as well. I was nothing without him, he told me. This was something he'd said often, jokingly, but now? Now it was meant to hurt. He prevented me from going out with my friends. At first, he would say it was because he wanted my company, but later I think he was afraid I might tell people what was happening. The more he drank and took drugs, the worse he became. He was swinging between being sorry—so, so sorry— and being cruel. But in the end, his apologies stopped, and he just became horrible. I was afraid, and yet outside our flat, he was still being Bruno, to dance, to charm the others.'

Her tears had started again. He could feel their dampness through his tee-shirt. He should have paid more attention a year ago and yet, by then, it was nearly the end of Bruno's career and the end of her suffering, too. It hadn't surprised him to read MetroCapital had released Bianchi shortly after the company's return to the United Kingdom. He'd seen the slip in Swan Lake, Lizzie's bruised arm and the glowering presence of the man himself, and together they added up to someone who was losing his grip.

'Why didn't you leave?'

'For a long time, I thought I'd be able to help him, but by the time I realised I couldn't, he was afraid of losing everything, so he turned to threats. If I exposed him, he said, he'd stop me dancing, too. He hated me talking to anyone else unless he was there, in case I said something. When I came to speak to you, he was angry, but it was good we didn't talk for very long, because it stopped him from hurting me.'

'Why would he do something like that? Why would he hurt you?' Anton's insides roiled, and he felt nauseous as he thought about what she'd had to live through, which had possibly been worse for her to bear because Bruno had once been a good man. The betrayal and loss must have been greater—it certainly would have been for him, if Beatrix changed in such an obscene way.

'He didn't often. Truly, he didn't, and he was still bitterly sorry, right up to the end, of doing that. Just occasionally, if he thought I was paying too much attention to another male principal or s-someone like you, he'd hit me. It was his fear I'd leave him. He was afraid of so much—me leaving, losing his position in the company, not being able to dance—but he wouldn't realise it was paranoia caused by his drinking and drug-taking.'

'But I saw your wrist. That wasn't caused by being hit.'

There was a long moment of silence before Lizzie spoke in a low, shame-faced voice.

'I was cross because he'd made a slip in the pas de deux and it had frightened me. He grabbed my wrist after I said I would have to tell someone. I tried to twist away, so it was my fault and—'

''Stop! You weren't to blame. Ever. It was not your mistakes or silliness or stupidity which caused him to be abusive. You—*you*, Lizzie—are a beautiful and very talented dancer and you did nothing to deserve what he did.'

'He wouldn't try to seek help, even though I begged him. That's what I could never understand. It was horrible the way he'd swing from anger to remorse, but *he wouldn't seek help.*'

'Yes,' agreed Anton sadly, 'it's often the case when someone is addicted. Even if they know their habits are causing harm to themselves and their loved ones, they will not stop. But I cannot understand why the company didn't notice sooner?'

'I think they had. They asked me a few times if everything was okay, and there was something about their look when they asked that made me wonder. And I think maybe Bruno suspected he was being watched, too. Then he messed up completely. He turned up to dance in Giselle, but it was clear he was drunk. The alternative lead took the role that night instead.'

'I'm glad you moved away from him, my Lizzie. He might have really hurt you.' There was a long silence as he continued to cradle her in his arms, his eyes fixed unseeingly on the sea as he ached for her. While the trouble she'd endured had been shorter lived than his, it was so much worse. Having someone you had once loved, laughed with, made love to, who descended into a self-created living hell, was so very sad. His family might not agree with his proposals, but they loved him, and, one day, he was certain they could sort out their differences.

Lizzie stirred and lifted her head. 'They conducted an enquiry, spoke to other company members. Many had become afraid of him by then. He blamed me, of course. He threatened if he went down, he'd take me with him.'

It was no wonder she'd lost confidence, and it was probably why the company had sent her here. Anton had already checked Tim Faversham out on the internet and found out where was from, which was too close to Mondorra for comfort. He also knew why he was dancing with the MetroCapital Outreach—because although an excellent dancer, he was untried on the international stage. So Tim could keep an eye on her when they were demonstrating or dancing, but he felt an uneasy fear settle in his stomach. If Bruno really was in Solhaven, he might follow Lizzie, and if he saw her alone, he might carry out his threat and harm her. But Lizzie had said—he was sure she'd said—that she'd not seen him since he'd left the company, and that must be nearly a year ago, now.

Anton stroked her hair, brushing it back from her tear-streaked face and tucking it behind her ears, overwhelmed with tenderness and a desire to look after her. She needed caring for, and he saw how it might be possible to protect her with no one being aware of it. He would have to get in touch with Paulo, head of his security detail. After all, they'd be bored at the moment, with him being absent from Mondorra. It was taking a risk, bringing them here, but the guys who worked in the detail knew they had to remain discreet. He'd hate to have this quiet place overrun with curiosity seekers. More especially, he didn't want his father finding out where he was and trying to persuade him home, probably by playing on his love for his parents and duty to Mondorra—but yet, not until he was ready to concede to modernisation and reform. The risk couldn't be avoided, because for now, Lizzie was more important, and it was a risk he was prepared to take.

Lizzie gave him a watery smile. 'Come, I've stopped crying now. Let's walk on. It's so beautiful here. I think—I think that's why I've suddenly let go. Haven House is indeed a haven, and I've met you again, which is unbelievable. Just now, in the café, Jake was so happy and it was so funny about the surf board in the bath with his little baby. I looked inside myself and saw the darkness still weighing me down and all the happiness and light around me. It just all spilled out from there.'

Anton held her back when she would have walked on and tilted her chin with his finger, dropping a gentle kiss on her lips, kissing each of her eyelids, which had fluttered closed, tasting the salt of her tears. He heard a soft moan escape her lips and felt her fingers on his shoulders, clinging to him.

'I'm here, Lizzie. I shall never leave you.' His words were a whispered promise as his mouth returned to hers, his tongue slipped inside, and they tasted each other.

Much as he would have liked to deepen the kiss further, he pulled back. This wasn't the time for pressing more emotion onto her. This was a time for support. The rest would come later... if she'd even consider having him when she knew who he was. It was a big ask, taking on the role of crown princess, even though his modernisations would lessen the pomp surrounding the royal family. But he knew he had to persuade her. She was becoming so important in his life.

'Come. Yes, let us continue with the walk. And tell me more, because I think there are still things which need to be said.'

Lizzie looked more relaxed as they turned towards the end of the beach. He slung his arm round her shoulder and held her close to his side, and after a few moments he felt her arm slide round his waist and caught his breath in sheer delight at her touch. Briefly he closed his eyes and saw her naked in his bed, arms stretched up towards him, a smile on her face and he—but enough! Such thoughts were causing his body to respond rather too obviously, and as he'd already decided this wasn't the time.

'There's not a lot more to tell. Before I walked out, I was a bit of a recluse. If I tried to go anywhere, it upset him. I kept hoping he'd wake up one day and realise he was destroying himself. I realised I didn't love him by then, but I would have stayed to see him through it if he'd chosen to quit. He told me he was the only partner who could make me look good on stage, and no-one else could ever love me. I think I hated him by then.' She shuddered.

Anton squeezed her shoulders. 'You know he was

wrong? Quite, quite wrong?' A warmth expanded in his chest, and he knew, finally and definitely, that he loved her.

'Yes, but after nearly two years of it, I was worn down and had begun to believe him. Then I saw you and, I don't know, it was so strange. Something called to me, stronger than my fear of Bruno, and I had to come and speak to you.'

'Ah, cherie, I'm so sorry. I wanted to talk to you much longer than we did, for I felt something spark between us, too, but I wasn't in a very good place. When you first arrived, you seemed to hang onto Bruno, and when you finally came to me, he was glowering at us both, so it seemed best to end our conversation. I'm so sorry. But if I had talked to you for any length of time, what then would have happened? Perhaps it was as well we didn't speak for long.'

'Yes, I know.' Lizzie fell silent and leaned her head against his shoulder. 'Anyway, I found some strength to fight back from that night onwards from something you said and—what? What did I just say?'

Her words had caused him to take a sharp breath, astonished by the coincidence. 'Oddly, I, too, found some strength that night, too. It was from you, and it was the very next day I told my father I could no longer continue as I was, and we had to change.' He glanced down at her and saw her small, contented smile.

'I'm happy you changed your life.'

'You said a life without a purpose wasn't good, or something similar.'

'And you told me I should get a new hairdryer!'

They walked on a few paces before Lizzie continued, her voice sad. 'I still feel guilty because I couldn't help him, even though I know there was nothing I could do. I'm still recovering from his two years of verbal abuse. He kept telling me I was unlovable and no good as a dancer. And I have a bit of fear inside because of his threats. Thinking I saw him this morning made that fear return.'

'There is no need for fear. I will make sure of your safety, that I promise. Will you believe me in this? It will take about a day to organise, but I have an idea.'

Lizzie stopped again, turning to Anton, her fists balled at her sides, cheeks flushed with unshed tears causing her eyes to glitter. 'I don't want you to put yourself in harm's way. Promise me that?'

The tears escaped her eyes and slowly trickled down her cheeks as Anton pulled her back into his embrace, hushing her, rocking her. 'Indeed no, Lizzie. I will not put myself in any danger at all. But... you must accept maybe it wasn't him you saw but just someone who looks a bit like him?'

He felt her nodding, heard her muffled words.

'I know.'

'This has been a heavy burden for you to bear and I think probably better out than held inside you, like poison in a wound. Now the wound can heal.'

Anton stared sightlessly over her head as he comforted her, his heart aching for everything she'd been through.

Later, much later that night, after they'd eaten, and

he'd seen her safely into the hotel, he phoned Paulo and told him what was required.

That done, he sat for a long time nursing a small whisky. He'd already acknowledged it would be a great deal to ask of Lizzie, to be his wife, but he was sure she would manage. His future was still uncertain, though, because at the very back of his mind was the rather terrifying thought his papa would never back down. He was only in his mid-fifties and could remain king for twenty years. Hah! There would be no Mondorra left, if things continued as they were.

For the very first time, Anton seriously thought about the alternative—to leave Mondorra permanently. The idea was jarring and made him feel uncomfortable, but… would he do that if Lizzie felt she couldn't become the crown princess?

He didn't think he could.. His country needed him. The people needed leadership and modernisation. If it came down to such a choice, he'd be torn in half. Either decision would leave him bleeding.

He sighed and drained the last few drops from his glass. He had to hope Bea was reading the situation correctly at home, and his father was discussing changes and would ask for his return.

And he had to hope Lizzie could see her way to being his wife.

CHAPTER 11

Lizzie felt happier, more confident. Anton made her feel valued. Wanted. Needed.

Odd they had both taken strength and inspiration from each other that night. It comforted her and made her feel closer to him.

Odd, too, how she could talk to him so freely, and not just about her troubles, either. When Anton had been satisfied she'd let go of all her misery and fear, their conversation moved on, became more general. They'd talked about music, ballet and art again. She'd found out more about his student days, when he'd come here for a surfing holiday two years running, looking for Jake Bradstock, only to learn later he'd been in plain sight the whole time. It tuned out he was quite an action man, too. They had a shared love of horses and horse riding, although Lizzie had to confess she'd not done much since she was a teenager and would love to spend some time honing her skills. But Anton also skied, kayaked and climbed.

Returning to the café, she'd felt starving. They'd eaten well, choosing a Moroccan curry which was fragrant and plentiful, before he'd driven her back to the hotel.

Sitting in his car, they'd drawn close, mouths softly gentle until passion had grown, then their lips had clung more fiercely and their hands had wandered more freely until Anton had gently pushed her away and pleaded for mercy. She was a little disappointed he didn't ask her back to his room, but he was being considerate. That after her outpouring, maybe making love wasn't a great idea.

Now, this morning, Lizzie sang in the shower then performed pas de chats back into the bedroom, a gleam in her eye, her mind lighter than it had been since that dreadful night when she'd walked out on Bruno. His poison had been growing weaker over the last few months, and by telling Anton everything she'd released the last of it... apart from one dark corner of her mind, which was her fear of him lurking somewhere, ready to carry out his threat. Especially now she thought she'd seen him.

Pushing that away, she dressed and ran down the beautiful staircase, remembering every time she descended what Emily had said about it on the day she'd arrived. Almost feeling like entering the dining-room with a full jete, she restrained herself and instead, walked in demurely and joined Tim at the small table they seemed to have appropriated for themselves.

'Good morning.' Tim smiled, looking surprised. 'You

seem different today. I don't think I've ever seen you like this.'

'No. But once I was like this all the time. Last night I had a long talk with Anton, and he drilled some sense into me and made me realise none of what happened with Bruno was my fault.' Lizzie was damned if she kept quiet about it anymore. While she'd never mention the worst, she was prepared to speak out about his drinking and drug taking.

'What happened with...? I don't understand.' Shaking his head, Tim reached for the teapot and poured them both some aromatic green tea. He'd also brought her a bowl of yogurt, fruit and muesli, and she assumed his preferred full English breakfast was on its way.

'Towards the end of our time together, Bruno had developed some bad habits.' She calmly explained about his problems and that he'd clung on to her too forcefully for it to be acceptable. 'Anton pointed out I wasn't responsible and Bruno was the only person who could have stopped it all.'

'So you've been sitting on all this guilt ever since? That's what's affected your dancing?'

'Yes. Wait. You'll see.'

She knew when they danced this afternoon, at a matinee in a town about twenty miles distant, that she would surprise Tim. The director and senior ballet master back at MetroCapital would have smiled and nodded their heads. Their ploy had worked and Lizzie was back. By some amazing chance, she'd found Anton again, too, by coming here. Yet there was still a mystery surrounding him, and she still wondered sometimes about his request not to tell anyone where they'd met. Surely his father wouldn't send someone after him?

The object of her thoughts appeared, walking across the travelled forecourt pushing a wheelbarrow loaded with garden tools, banishing her suspicion. She smiled. He looked relaxed and happy in scruffy jeans and a faded blue tee shirt with a tear on one shoulder.

Tim's breakfast arrived, and he set to with relish. Lizzie knew he would already have been for a run and done at least fifty push-ups since he got up, so his appetite was justified.

'Do you miss France?'

'*Pourquoi*? There is no reason for me to miss it. After all, I can go home when I have spare time, and I might not stay with MetroCapital anyway. I don't have the drive or ambition to become a renowned ballet dancer. I might go back to Paris.' His smile was self-mocking as he looked up at her, some bacon and mushroom speared on his fork.

From the corner of her eye, Lizzie noticed Anton stop. She twisted her head to see him more clearly. He took his phone out of his back pocket, glanced at the screen and pressed to accept his call. This was the first time she'd seen him with a phone.

'Lizzie?' Tim looked up, saw Anton out of the window and grinned. 'You've got it bad.'

'I saw him just under a year ag—' She stopped, horrified. She'd been about to tell Tim where they'd met. That's what came when you put down your burden of always watching what you said and who you spoke to. It made you careless. Damn. 'In class. And he came several times, but we didn't speak much. Then I never saw him again until we came here. Such a coincidence.'

She was prattling, so she glanced back out of the window and saw the exact moment Anton froze, clearly listening carefully to the person on the other end of the phone call, then he gesticulated and ended the call, thrusting it into his pocket before rubbing his chin and standing motionless. He hadn't liked whatever he'd heard, that was for sure. Within a minute, he squared his shoulders and strode towards the front entrance.

'Oops,' Tim commented. 'That wasn't welcome news.'

At that moment the coach nosed onto the gravel sweep, and the dancers stood up to drift out to their transport, bags hanging from their shoulders, talking of the day's itinerary. Tim grabbed a last mouthful of bacon and poured the rest of his coffee into a travel mug, then he and Lizzie followed the others out.

Anton stood by the reception desk, talking quietly to Emily and casually flipping through the pile of newspapers and magazines delivered daily to the hotel. Lizzie shot him a curious look, disappointed he didn't turn to acknowledge her, for he must have known the dancers were leaving—no other guests went out in such numbers at the same time each morning, after all.

Was he telling Emily about his phone call? Did he have a problem?

Pausing, she continued to watch. After a few more flips, his shoulders sagged, and he drew one magazine out. Emily smiled, said something in reply, and turned to answer the ringing phone. Anton twisted away, the magazine in his hand. He stopped dead when he saw Lizzie, his lips compressing, eyes flicking to the side before his gaze returned to meet her steady look. He glanced down and looked at his hand holding the folded magazine loosely next to his thigh, then he returned his gaze to her, his mouth opening as if he was going to speak before closing again.

'Hi, Anton.' She waited. She wouldn't question him. She'd had enough persistent questions from Bruno about what she was doing and where she was going ever to inflict that on someone else. And indeed, what did she expect him to say, other than he'd had a phone call which had upset him and he'd come inside to collect a magazine? She was reading far too much into it. Except for his reaction to the call and his sudden rush inside, when prior to that he'd been sauntering along with the tools of his job, clearly looking forward to a day spent in the gardens.

'Lizzie?' Tim came back inside, looking puzzled until he saw Anton. 'Oh! Sorry, am I interrupting? But Lizzie, the coach is ready to go. We have a demonstration class in an hour, and we need to get there in time to change and warm up, okay?' Turning, he shot out of the door again.

'Yes. Sorry, Tim. I'm on my way. Anton, have a good day and thanks again for listening yesterday.'

As if his feet had unglued themselves, Anton moved forward. 'Lizzie, so lovely to see you.' His eyes were warm as he reached out and, unseen by Emily, gently touched his fingers to her lips.

'Is everything okay? Only I saw you had a phone call and you seemed a bit upset about it.' She shrugged her shoulders, annoyed with herself for giving in to the urge to ask. 'I couldn't help but see. You were right outside the windows.'

'Oh, it was my friend updating me about something, and then I remembered there was a magazine I needed to pick up.'

He shrugged dismissively, but she saw a faint flush of red running along his cheekbones, and his eyes briefly dropped to study the black and white tiled floor for a second time before he looked up, breaking into a wide smile. 'A bonus to see you. But you must go. Dance well, my swan princess. Maybe I can meet you later this evening?'

He turned her gently towards the door and walked out with her, watching as she got on the coach before turning back to his wheelbarrow.

Lizzie shook her head, craning her neck as the coach turned and slowly set off up the drive.

Why did she feel he hadn't been completely truthful?

Yet this was the man who'd set her free. His gentleness, calm demeanour, and patience had wrapped her in a blanket of comfort and safety where she'd felt able to spill out all the poison of those last months with Bruno.

Lizzie sank back in her seat. There was a lot she didn't know about Anton, other than he came from Mondorra and had a mysterious father, and also had a burning desire to modernise the family company.

Yet she trusted him completely, felt complete when she was with him, could talk to him about anything.

It would be good to know exactly what had upset him this morning, though, and whether the magazine had some bearing on it. She hadn't been able to see what it was. Maybe it was a report about his company and he hadn't wanted anyone to see it? Couldn't he have told her, if that was the case?

Because she was certain the magazine was tied in somehow, and the reason for him being upset had come from that, and not the friend's phone call.

How was it possible to remain so certain of his integrity? What was the full extent of the problems with his father and his company? Her mind was conflicted. She hoped in time he'd explain everything in full, but as he'd not pushed her, she didn't want to push him. She needed the same patience he'd shown, except she still felt somewhat fragile with trusting again.

CHAPTER 12

ANTON WAITED for the coach to arrive back at the hotel. He swore quietly under his breath as he thought about their earlier encounter. At some point he had to tell Lizzie what his "job" really was, that his father was the king, but the time wasn't yet right. She was just emerging from being the frightened and subdued woman created by Bruno, and he needed to let her grow before throwing something this momentous at her. There were things he'd not sorted out in his own mind, too. Did she love him as much as he loved her? If she did, would it be enough for her to accept his position? What could be done to merge her career with her duties if she accepted his proposal? He also needed to have his future more settled, get this business with his father sorted out and sorted soon.

The list was overwhelming, and all the points needed careful thought.

He'd even considered never returning, but he knew he couldn't, however tempted he might be. Duty would win. It had been instilled in him since birth and was a part of who he was. And not just duty, either—he loved his country, and he wanted the best for it and knew he had much to offer.

But for the first time in his life, he was in love. In love like Jake and Emily. In love like Claire and Daniel. The *idea* of being in love with Lizzie had been with him a long time. To find her, spend time with her, and still be in love with her was even better. In fact, it was incredible, and he didn't want to lose her. She was fun to be with, and they had many things in common. She listened and discussed. She knew when to be quiet, and she had a lovely way with people.

So what would he do if she wouldn't return with him as the crown princess? The enormity of it worried him and prompted him to consider the impossible—throw it all up for her. Rubbing his hand over his face, his mind was full of ifs and buts and his head ached. He rotated his shoulders and stretched, trying to dispel his tension.

It had been Bea, ever faithful as a sister, as a friend, who'd rung that morning. She wanted to warn him of something she'd been told by one of her friends at the newly-established refuge. An article in one of the monthly gossip magazines, titled "Missing Celebs—Where Are They Now?" and which included a photo and some wild supposition about Prince Maximilian.

Distaste curled his lip, and a cold shudder ran through him at his close escape. As soon as the call was disconnected, he recalled seeing that same magazine several times before, in the hotel sitting-room, and had gone inside in search of it. Now, it was hidden in his room, and all he could hope was Emily hadn't noticed its absence and called the newsagent for a replacement.

It had been a shock to turn and see Lizzie, and he knew she'd seen him take the magazine and was curious why, so now he waited for her. He wanted to see her anyway, to tell her why he'd acted so oddly. His stomach churned, and he fisted his hands so hard he felt his fingernails bite into his palms.

His heart picked up speed as the long white vehicle nose out from under the avenue of trees. She was on board, maybe looking for him, maybe feeling eager to see him.

She was the last to vacate the coach, and he saw her glance round and smile, when she saw him

Stepping forwards, all his doubts and worries fled. A lightness filled him, and his heart beat faster, as it usually did when he saw her. Suddenly everything seemed possible. Everything would work out. He was sure of it. He picked her up and swung her round, uncaring of any eyes which might see them from the dining-room. As he set her down, he kissed her, and the thrill of lust speared through him, his body responding to the feel and warmth of her. 'Lizzie, my swan princess. Have you had a good day? Do you think you have danced more freely because now you are rid of the pain?'

Lizzie smiled, her hands resting on his shoulders. 'Such a greeting! Yes, yes. I danced better than I've done for a very long time. I hadn't realised how Bruno's behaviour had worn me down, but it's been a long time since I took such joy from my dancing. I don't know what made me approach you at the palace, but there was something stronger than either of us at work that night.' Her face sobered. 'You can't know how often I have conjured you up in my mind and clung to you since I walked out on Bruno, taking strength from you and your words. I should have told you that, last night.'

He wrapped her in his arms. 'And do you know, you were the final trigger to my rebellion. You were my inspiration, my poster girl. I wanted to meet you again, but it was important to meet you on equal ground.'

She laughed. 'You mean neutral ground, don't you?'

Well, no, he didn't, but it would do for now. He most definitely hadn't wanted to meet her as Prince Maximilian. That was all that really mattered here, although quite how he was going to untangle everything, he wasn't sure. If she saw the magazine and flicked through it, maybe when she was in Solhaven, he'd be lost, because it didn't paint him in a very good light. The photos had all come from a period in his life when he'd backed off from nagging his father.

He hoped for two things—that she hadn't seen which magazine he'd picked up, and that she was the sort who probably wouldn't look at it anyway. At least his photos were hidden well inside. The cover featured some film star. But whereas once there was no urgency to explain everything, now there was, because she'd moved from someone he was interested in, to someone he loved. And she deserved the truth.

'What would you like to do tonight, Lizzie?'

'I'm tired. I've danced with my heart, and I'm tired. Can we eat here?' She wore a look of uncertainty.

'It will be very pleasant to eat here with you. I often eat my evening meal in the hotel, but it's been rather lonely. I usually bring a book with me. Will I intrude on your group? Will they want to pull the performance to pieces or talk about what is planned for tomorrow?'

'We pulled the performance to pieces in the coach on our way back, but there wasn't a lot of pulling needed, to be honest. We were all pleased. William's already run through tomorrow's commitments after the class this morning. Do you mind not going elsewhere?'

'Not at all. You will want to shower. I shall wait for you in the sitting-room and admire my handiwork through the windows.'

Within half an hour, he saw Lizzie slip into the lounge, casually dressed in a skirt and short-sleeved top in yellow. She fitted in well with the beautiful room, which was painted in cream, picked out in gilt, and scattered with comfortable groups of chairs and settees. She crossed the floor with such grace of movement it caused his breath to catch in his throat. That this beautiful woman might one day be his was a stunning thought. But—and here his mind returned to the massive problem which dominated his every waking moment—what would she think of the necessity to marry, and marry with all the pomp and ceremony Mondorra was capable of? He shook his head slightly and stood as she approached. Stepping forwards, he greeted her with a kiss on each cheek—perhaps a more thorough kiss than he would normally give someone when formally greeting them, but it was a "we are in public" salutation, rather than the ardent kiss he wanted to give her. His eyes must have betrayed his passion, because a blush crept over her cheeks, and her pulse fluttered in her throat.

'A drink?'

'Iced water, please.'

The server came across and within moments Lizzie had an iced water and he had a small whisky.

'Lizzie, I need to speak to you. I think this morning you wondered what I was doing, because you were right in what you said, about the call and rushing inside—'

Lizzie held her hand up. 'I'd forgotten it, to be honest. There was a lot going on today and it was my first performance with Tim, dancing as I used to. Don't feel you have to explain every move to me. There's no place for suspicion and guilt in a friendship... a relationship...?' Her voice hesitated with the last word.

Anton nodded and tried to find words in his own mind to describe what was happening inside him. He finally, and weakly, compared it to the New Year's Eve royal firework display, laughing at himself as he did. He pulled in a deep breath and huffed it out. Then, with joy dancing in his eyes, he reached out and caught her hand in his, running his fingers over her palm and wrist. He was reacting to her with every sense he had. Hopefully, his erection wouldn't be an embarrassment when they went into the dining-room.

'A *relationship*? Oh, yes. I would like that very much. But it makes it even more important I should explain a little.'

'Only if you want. I'm not asking. If we have no trust, there's no hope for us, and you know what? I think there's a hell of a lot of hope.'

Anton looked at her, and the glow within become even more intense. He spent a few moments absorbing his sheer happiness before he spoke about the call, an unpleasant necessity in view of what he was then going to tell her. 'The call was from a dear friend. She'd seen an article in a magazine about the... organisation I work for, and in it, the writer wondered where the second-in-command had gone, and whether there was anything wrong. She thought I ought to know anyway, but I knew the magazine was delivered here and I was concerned there would be a photo of me and it would link me to Mondorra, so I wanted to remove it. It was not honest of me to remove it from under Emily's nose like I did, but I didn't know what else to do.'

One photo? There had been at least six, all of which made him out to be a playboy—water-skiing, skiing, dancing with Beatrix, riding his horse, in a dinner jacket at some formal banquet. The article wondered where he was, why he'd not been seen doing any of the things shown in the photos, why he'd not attended certain state events by the side of his parents? Was he ill, and the king had not wanted to tell his people? In disgrace? All the usual drivel these magazines scraped up from remarkably little. Except he *had* disappeared, and no-one was saying where to or why.

Oh, how ironic, because it was a possibility the same magazine would soon beat on the palace door for exclusive rights to his wedding. The fee would be astronomical. He could donate it to the children's hospital.

Lizzie leaned forwards and dropped a soft kiss on his lips, and he dragged himself away from his daydream, back to Wales and his swan princess.

'I can understand,' Lizzie said consolingly. 'I thought it might be something like that—linking you to Mondorra.'

For a moment he wondered what she understood, then he came back down to earth and remembered he'd just explained about the magazine.

'Come. I'm hungry, and I suspect you are as well. Let's eat. And I want to ask you something.' His voice was serious, and Lizzie gave him a puzzled look as he took her hand and led her through the double doors to the dining-room.

They chose a window table overlooking the gravelled forecourt and manicured, formal beds, with a sweep of green lawn rising to clusters of trees on the horizon, where the drive emerged.

Once they'd ordered, Anton offered wine and at Lizzie's shake of her head, poured himself a small glass. He swirled the golden liquid and took a small sip before replacing it on the table where he rotated it round and round, staring at the light sparkling through it, wondering what to say. Shaking his head, he focused on Lizzie, who was telling him about the class, and the performance in the afternoon when she and Tim had danced a pas de deux from Don Quixote.

'Tim was surprised afterwards.' Lizzie laughed. 'It's the first time he's danced with the proper me, the real me. He commented on how light I was, which made me laugh. And it's you I have to thank for that.'

'It would have happened eventually.'

She looked serious. 'I'm not so sure. My sister hasn't been able to get through, and neither did the counsellor I was seeing. But I feel as if I've known you a long time, that we have no secrets from each other.'

Anton shifted in his chair and looked out at the tranquil scene, his hand fiddling with the knife next to his side plate. No secrets. His shoulders sagged as he expelled a long breath. Okay, he'd explained—sort of—about the magazine, but there was so much more he needed to say He sat back as their starter arrived.

'These tomatoes taste wonderful,' Lizzie enthused as she cut a juicy chunk from a slice, added a morsel of mozzarella cheese and popped the whole into her mouth.

'They are sent up every day, fresh. We grow them in the greenhouse. You must come down and see, sometime. We grow quite a lot of the vegetables, but we really will have to get some more help because there is too much to be done by just two people when you consider the restoration project as well. Just looking after the vegetables will soon be a full-time job.'

'Restoration of the gardens? Oh, yes! I remember you told me about it.'

'Mmm, but it will take them many years. You'll have seen the fountain now in the centre of the forecourt?'

'Yes, and it's pretty.' Lizzie nodded and took another mouthful.

'That wasn't there at all when I arrived. We found

the remains of the steps forming the support for the basin, then from the plans, we knew where the piping should go. Claire found a very similar basin from a reclamation yard, I think she called it, and now? We have a fountain!'

'That's lovely. Like the Cornish gardens.'

'I believe so.' There was a brief silence as Anton put his knife and fork neatly side by side on the plate, then pinned her with his gaze. He had to say something, he really did. 'Lizzie… if I went back to my organisation in Mondorra, and if things work out between us… would you consider joining me there?'

'But what if you never go back?'

'I think I have to go back.' His voice was sad.

'But if your father won't change things?'

'One day, my father will *have* to go and it will then be up to me to make the changes. I'd rather go back with an agreement in place, that he will let me make them now, but if he won't… I don't know. I felt terrible about leaving him, even though I had to make my point, make him understand just how serious I am about this. I feel a great sense of duty, too. A responsibility. Once, I wondered if I might walk away forever, but there is too much from the past to just throw it all away.'

Lizzie frowned, her head tilted as she listened. 'You still sound indecisive.'

'I am, yes, but only about *when* to return. It would be so much easier if…' his voice broke off before he took in a gulp of air and continued. 'You and I, we have both had our troubles. I think yours have been worse than mine, and you have coped with them admirably and kept on, even though your heart was stifled. Me, I have simply run away. Yes, it was to force the acceptance of unwelcome reforms, but I still have not got word that things will be different. I'm reluctant to go back just yet. I'll give it more time, but one day, I have decided—*one day*—I must return. So... would you consider coming with me?'

It was bad enough, asking her to leave the country of her birth, but what of her career, also? How would they manage that? He hesitated to tell her the whole of it just yet. That even should his changes be implemented, she would be the centre of attention wherever she went and she'd be expected to undertake some sort of charitable work. Her life would, of necessity, be more controlled than it ever had been. It seemed glamorous from the outside, and things *would* get better, but still... when you hadn't been raised to it, it would be hard to adjust.

He'd come here for some peace, and a chance to reflect while he hoped his father would finally realise how he felt. He hadn't expected to re-encounter Lizzie and fall in love with her. Now he must tell her of his future role, and soon, but he'd not fully come to grips with it, constantly worried about the whole mess. What on earth would her reaction be when he told her who he was? What would her reaction be when he told her he could face his future better, knowing she was by his side?

Lizzie stared at him. This whole evening was turning out to be a lot more subdued than he'd intended. Dropping his eyes, he pushed his plate away and picked up his wine glass, suddenly fascinated with the golden liquid inside as it picked up the lights of the room. He was aware of the murmured conversations and occasional laughter of the other guests even as he thought about his question.

Would she return with him to Mondorra?

From under his lashes, he saw her brows drawn into a frown as she leaned back in her chair. He'd love to go to bed with her, have her slim fingers trace patterns over his body, touching him as delicately as he'd seen her hands fluttering when she danced. The very thought caused his nipples to tense and a warmth to pool inside, making him restlessly shift on his chair, his jeans suddenly becoming uncomfortably tight. It wasn't just lust, though. He loved talking to her. She had a wide knowledge of many things, and an easy laugh. They shared a deep love of ballet, music, and books. He'd once mentioned riding. She liked it too, and it would be amazing to go out with her. She'd also said, and he completely agreed, she felt she'd known him forever, on a deeper level than the meeting of minds and exchanged kisses.

Taking a long sip from her glass, Lizzie set it carefully back down onto the pristine white cloth and took a deep breath. Anton sat up and turned to her, his face anxious.

'I think I could come to Mondorra with you, but there would need to be a lot of discussion. Discussion about my dancing, and the security of your job, for your father might end up throwing you out. In which case, where would we live, and what would I do once I stopped dancing? I've always wanted to open my own company, but teaching at a ballet school would be an alternative. I've discovered I enjoy teaching. Oh!' Lizzie flung up her hands and blew out a breath. 'It seems silly thinking about all that sort of thing when we should concentrate on each other, on love.'

'I have much relief that you will consider it, and I'm certain we can work things out.'

Lizzie laughed.

'What? How have I amused you? This is serious things, I would have you realise!' Anton relaxed and laughed, his eyes crinkling, enjoying the more humourous note which had crept into their exchange.

'Nothing. Truly, nothing. You were just a little mixed up is all.'

He eyed her for another few seconds before settling back down into his chair, a dazed look on his face. 'Thank you. But… you may yet change your mind.'

Once he told her, and she maybe backed away, what then? Others had given up crowns for love. Could *he* do that? The alternative was to rule without her by his side. Would it all seem sterile, empty and pointless without her supporting him, cheering him on? He knew he wanted the chance to improve his country and take it into the twenty-first century and was sure he could do this, but it would be much harder without Lizzie. Her wish to run a ballet school heartened him—that dream, at least, he could fulfill.

The other alternative—leaving his country for love of her—was at the moment one he didn't want to think about.

CHAPTER 13

THE SUMMER DAYS DRIFTED PAST, Lizzie becoming more and more liberated as she rediscovered her abilities and confidence. She and Anton had, by some silent agreement, stopped discussing the future and just lived for each day, when every evening, they would walk and talk. But now there was more, much more growing between them. A few kisses were no longer enough for Lizzie, and she suspected for Anton as well, but he was forever the restrained and perfect gentleman, who saw her every night to the door of the hotel, never pushing things, ignoring the fact that as they'd kissed on the beach, in the car or in the gardens, his erection had been hard against her, making her catch her breath with longing, making her want to free it from its painful prison and for them both to enjoy some skin on skin love-making.

Anton only needed to look at her with those green eyes of his, shot through with gold, which spoke of his love. He only had to give her his half smile as he tugged her hand so they ran with the wind along the empty beach in the evening. Or when he held out his fork for her to try whatever he'd chosen, laughing when she hesitated. All those things and more caused her insides to dissolve into a pool of desire, and when he held her hips, stroked his hands down her back or cupped her jaw as he ravished her mouth, she was completely lost. She would go to her lonely bedroom and toss and turn until her body had cooled down sufficiently to allow her to sleep. Thanks to the hard work of their outreach days, this fortunately didn't take too long. She'd wait no longer. If he wouldn't instigate the next step, then she damn well would!

It had to be soon, because the idyllic days spent demonstrating and performing would eventually end, and they would have to return to London, although Lizzie had been thinking about taking a two-week break and staying at Haven House as a private guest. It would depend on MetroCapital and their plans for her. Except the autumn programme would already be underway. If they wanted her to take a leading role, it would be in spring, and rehearsals wouldn't start for a while.

She hardly dared contemplate the alternative—that their summer paradise would soon end. They'd still not discussed the future, apart from him asking her if she'd be prepared to return, one day, to Mondorra with him, followed by his rather cryptic comment that she might change her mind.

Why would she do that? Ever since that conversation, they'd strengthened the bond between them, spent most of their free time together, were accepted as a couple by both the dancers and the hotel staff.

Maybe he hadn't realised their time here was nearly over? He would soon, because their final presentation was next Saturday night. Then they had a few days free and would return to London the following Wednesday.

The rest of the week flew past. Their day of the last evening performance arrived. It was held in the local high school gym and was packed not only with staff and guests from the hotel but also with locals and tourists. As Lizzie took her final bows, an enormous bouquet of hothouse flowers was presented to her. Stunned, she looked round, wondering who had sent them. Maybe the company had heard about her recovery? Of course, the company would have heard—William would have kept them informed. But… it was strange, considering their location. She risked a quick glance at the stiff, gold-edged card tucked amongst the rose. "Fly high. Fly free."

They must be from Anton! How sweet. How lovely of him. But then she felt worried. After all the doubts Bruno had sown, worrying was not surprising. What did he mean, *"fly free"*?

No. All he meant was she should move forwards, free of all her burdens. That was all. Since talking to him, spilling it all out, she'd been able to do that, without a doubt.

Sunday arrived. Anton suggested, once her daily classes were finished, they could visit a beach a few miles distant. Like many of the stunning beaches in the area, access was by foot.

The drive only took them half an hour and they parked behind a rather stony beach, attractive in its own right, with an occasional cottage dotted about which stood testimony to fishermen of days gone past. Or maybe quarry workers, because shortly after climbing to the top of the cliff, they looked down into a deep blue lagoon, encircled by cliffs and rocks which was, Anton told her, an old slate quarry.

'Goodness, it seems dangerous taking slate out so close to the sea.' Lizzie leaned forwards to gaze in awe at the shimmering depths, and Anton caught hold of her arm.

'I don't know, but I think they maybe broke the last circle of rock after they'd finished quarrying. I'm only making a guess at this, you understand?'

'It must have been quite hard loading it into boats, too,' Lizzie said thoughtfully as they continued along the cliff path.

'They took it across land on a tramway to another little port further up the coast. It's a place worth visiting because it has a lot of old buildings which were used for slate and bricks as well.'

'You seem to know a lot about the area?'

He pulled her to a stop and kissed her, causing her pulse to thrum. 'Before I devoted all my time to you, I explored all the nearby coast. Some, I remember from when I came as a student, but much was new to me. Jake and Claire told me of places to go, for they have lived here all their lives.'

They had views along the coast in every direction. The sea was green and blue and flecked with white caps while clouds raced across the sky, dappling both land and water with speeding shadows. Their path led round the edge of a meadow before running between a raised bank on the seaward side and a wire fence to prevent trespass between them and fields. The verges on either side were full of bit scabious, thrift, sorrel, ox-eye daisies and both white and pink campion. A lark sang, lost somewhere in the blue height of the sky. If anyone was looking for perfection, Lizzie thought, as they walked along hand in hand, this surely had to be it.

They reached a slight dip in the path and at the bottom of the dip, some metal steps led down—not quite vertical, but nearly so—and they needed care. At the bottom were rocks to their right and a beach stretching out to their left, with more rocks than Haven Bay, but plenty of sand as well, to cater for the castle builders and frisbee players, of whom there was a scattering.

'Come.' Anton beckoned, and she raised her eyebrows, because he was moving to the right, towards a small cleft between two towering rocks.

'Come,' he repeated. 'This you can do.'

He was right—the cleft was about four feet from beginning to end, but it was possible to place her feet on pieces of flat-topped rock running through the gap, and when Anton lifted her down at the other end, Lizzie looked up and gasped. If she'd thought the day was already magical, it became even more so as she saw a small, secret beach in front of her. Not as sandy as the main beach, and not as big, but scattered with rocks and backed by high, honey-coloured cliffs. It was a sheer delight. The waves tumbled and frothed onto the beach and there was no-one else except themselves as they explored it all.

Sitting in a sheltered spot out of the wind, leaning back against one of the tilted rocks which seemed a feature of the beaches round here, Anton delved into his rucksack and produced a picnic he'd acquired from Jeff in the kitchen. A few gulls circled overhead before settling onto the sand a short distance away, strutting back and forth, with a beady yellow eye constantly fixed on the sandwiches they ate.

Idly throwing some bread, Lizzie laughed as they cried out and pounced, the lucky winner sweeping skywards, being chased by the others in a vain hope they might steal the prize.

'Which is silly,' Lizzie said, 'because if they stayed, I would have thrown more bread for them. I'm stuffed, Anton. But…'

'But what, my Lizzie?' Anton trailed a finger over her cheek, almost making it impossible to think.

She rolled over until she was in his arms, and his lips came down to cover hers. Joy singing in her heart, she kissed sensuously, her tongue dancing with his, arching to the caress of his hands which today travelled to places he'd previously denied himself. Shamelessly, she slid down her zip so he could access her body more easily, and allowed her own hand to trail over the hardness of his penis, undoing his own zip, touching her hand to the velvet softness at the tip, moist and ready.

Her breath rushed out of her body and all she wanted was to complete the removal of the barrier of their clothes. Oh, sweet agony—he touched her centre, and she bucked in response, a moan deep in her throat. But not here. Not here where at any moment someone else might find their secret cove. She needed them to go back to the hotel and then his room, her room—she didn't care, only knew that the time had come. The whole, beautiful day had led to now, to this moment… and was going to lead them further.

'Anton… Anton… can we go back? Please, can we go back?'

He knew. He knew what she meant, what she wanted. She didn't have to explain. Boneless, she watched as he packed up his rucksack, dusted the sand from his jeans, and held out his hand to pull her up.

In silence, they crossed back to the main beach and trod up the steps.

In silence, they walked back to the car.

In silence, they drove to the hotel.

Sitting in the car, the engine ticking as it cooled, Anton looked at her. 'Lizzie, this isn't something I take lightly. I have asked you, if I went back to Mondorra, would you come with me? I need to tell you something more—'

Even though her heart leapt in relief that he'd not backed away from asking her to go with him, she cut him off. 'No! I'm tired of talking. My problems, your problems—damn them all to hell. I want this afternoon to be about us! I want your body naked against mine. I want to feel you inside, filling me. I want to have an orgasm, and see you come as well.'

Lizzie trembled as he looked at her for a long moment, before sighing. The sigh was followed by a tender smile, and he opened his door. 'Come.'

He led her into the cool darkness of the garage and up a flight of wooden steps to unlock a door leading to a large airy room. It was bedroom, sitting-room, dining-room and kitchen all in one, and a further door beyond the bed led, she assumed, to an ensuite.

Locking the door, he leaned back against it and opened his arms. 'Come.'

She went into his arms with a small sob, her emotions tumbling around inside, her longing dominating them all. But there was also a deep sense of coming home, of being with the right person, of having stopped looking.

After the time spent on the beach, it only took moments for the flames to re-ignite as Anton kissed her mouth, his hands steadily unfastening the buttons of her shirt. Releasing her hold of him, he pulled it off and dropped it on the floor, followed immediately by his tee shirt. Her bra was next, and she pressed her breasts against his sun-bronzed chest, lean and muscled.

Walking her backwards even as he continued to kiss her, he laid her down on the bed and knelt to undo and remove her jeans. His mouth teased and worshipped her as she clutched his hair, her hips rising to ease his access. She whimpered, her guttural cries rising in a crescendo until she shrieked out his name.

They lay, his head on her thigh, until her tremors had died.

'Anton, please, I need you inside me.'

Her plea galvanised him to stand and pull off his jeans and boxer briefs. Finally, she could see and touch what had been tantalising her for so many days. With near reverence, she touched the tip of his penis and revelled in his harsh intake of breath as it leapt under her seeking fingers. His face a mask of love and longing, he searched in the drawer of the small bedside cabinet and dug out a foil packet, which he ripped open with his teeth.

'You better not touch me too much,' he warned. 'I've been dreaming about you just about every night. You'll make me come, doing that. Wait. Wait.'

Within seconds he was poised over her, ready to enter, to find his own release and give her the atavistic pleasure of him deep inside. His thrusts were slow, his fingers active, and when Lizzie arched up for a second time, he lost himself in her, his shout mingling with hers as they both embraced their climax.

CHAPTER 14

LYING ON HIS BACK, sated after several bouts of lovemaking, most of them slower and gentler than their first frantic coupling, Anton looked troubled. He'd tried to tell Lizzie who he was when they'd been sitting in the car, but she'd refused to do any more talking. He understood why, understood she wanted loving. No ifs, no buts—just loving. And hell, so did he. He'd been yearning for her ever since they'd re-connected.

He had to tell her soon, but to go back to Mondorra as the Crown Princess was a hell of a lot to ask of her. And always, it came back to her career. He'd seen her dance with Bruno, and, more recently, with Tim, and there was no doubt of it—she was a brilliant dancer. Even better now she'd shaken off Bruno's unkindness. She had more years at the top before considering another career and family.

On Wednesday, only the day after tomorrow, she was leaving. Of that, he was only too well aware.

He twisted his head to look at his watch, couldn't see

the face, stretched his free arm across their entwined bodies and hooked it up. Half-past six. Time, definitely, for him to be getting up, and also, he suspected, her. The coach usually left at eight-thirty, to take them to Solhaven town hall for their daily class, and she'd want to shower, get across to her own room and get into her practice clothes, and have breakfast. His sigh was heavy and blew tendrils of her hair away from her face.

'Lizzie. Lizzie, sweetheart.' Anton gently shook her, and she moaned, turned over with her back to him and buried her head in the pillow. 'Come on. You've got to leave for morning class in less than two hours.'

He was continually awed by the dedication to practice the dancers had. Did they ever miss class, go on holiday, or allow themselves to be ill? He intended to ask Lizzie if she might consider staying on after the outreach group went back to London. Surely she was allowed some holiday? But even if she stayed, she'd be up every morning and performing the barre exercises, at least. He could build her a barre, but where could it go? Back in Mondorra, she could have a whole damn ballet school if she wanted.

'Lizzie.'

'Go 'way! You've worn me out.'

Laughing, he went to have a shower, singing as he stood under the hot water. He'd never felt happier. He knew what put the smile on Jake's face when Emily entered a room. He knew why Claire had been almost dancing round the gardens after Daniel's return. With Lizzie at his side, he could almost face his father's intransigence again, and this time make him damn well agree to the reforms. But it would be so much better if his papa would send word and ask him to come back so they could work together and change things for the better. Then his cup would indeed be full—brim full.

Once dressed, Anton brewed coffee and took a mug to Lizzie, who still slept in the rumpled bed, dappled by the sun pouring in through the skylight.

'Get up. You've got class in just over an hour, my swan princess. You need your breakfast. All I can offer is coffee and toast, so if you're quick, we can go across and have breakfast together.'

They were soon seated in the hotel dining room, the other dancers drifting in without the usual sense of urgency and chatter. Tim came over, but Anton noticed Lizzie flicked him a glance, causing him to grin and move to another group on another table.

'Are you working today?'

'No, sweet Lizzie. I have arranged with Claire to take the time off and will work next Saturday to make it up, although she said I didn't need to do that. When your class is finished, I would like to talk to you. There are important things we need to discuss and sort out.' He stretched out his hand and took hold of hers.

He saw by her face she was concerned about his serious tone, especially after the night they'd just spent together, but what he had to say *was* serious, and he was terrified she'd turn away from who he was and what his "job" was. Anton sighed heavily, but although sometimes tempted to make his current situation as a gardener permanent, he couldn't and he wouldn't. He'd spent many long nights awake thinking about it all.

When his year here was up, he'd go back... unless his papa asked him to return before that.

Lizzie joined the throng of dancers as they left, and he sat, sadly watching her go, pretending to catch the kiss she blew just as she went out of the door. Maybe the last kiss she'd ever give him. He didn't doubt her love, but what he was asking of her was a great deal. Anton knew he must tell her before Wednesday and that might mean the end. Not of their love, perhaps, for he was certain that was as enduring as that of Siegfried and Odette, but of their future as a couple.

Enough! He straightened his shoulders. Enough of his misery and worry. If their love was so strong, there had to be a way forward.

It was later, hands in his pockets as he wandered aimlessly in the rose garden waiting for the coach to bring his Lizzie back, when a helicopter flew low overhead. He was keeping Claire company while she removed moss from a sundial with painstaking care, and they'd been talking about how soon they could get another of the fountains put back, this time in the centre of what would become the scented garden.

Claire squinted up into the bright sunlight. 'Ah yes. The helicopter.'

'What is it? Some sort of rescue?'

'No. Emily said someone had rung last night and asked if there was room for a helicopter to land. She reckoned yes, to one side of the drive, and gave permission as long as they emailed a waiver through saying the hotel wouldn't be held responsible for anything that happened... which apparently, they did.

She won't say who it was. Said if she blabbed about stuff like this, it'd give the hotel a bad name. All very hush hush. A flying visit!' She threw back her head, laughing. 'Some celeb checking us out for a holiday, do you think?'

Anton went still and his heart lurched. Was this something to do with him? Surely not! But… it could be.

Emily strode round the corner of the hotel, shading her eyes. Then she turned to someone behind her and pointed, called Claire and asked her if she could spare a moment.

Then he was left alone in the centre of the rose garden as Beatrix walked down the steps from the terrace towards him.

'Beatrix!' His heart was in his mouth, coldness seeping into his bones. 'Mama? Papa? They are well?' Fear laced his voice, and his hands trembled.

'Fear not, my friend. All is well. Your papa has sent a letter. When I heard it was so important it was being delivered by an official who would be transported by helicopter, I decided to be naughty! I have been curious about where you're living, so I offered to bring the letter and come to have a look. I can stay a few short days, and you can show me everything. It looks so beautiful.'

'And how did he know where to send it?'

'He asked me, Max. He told me it had to be delivered into your hand and was a fair letter, so I gave in and let him know about the hotel and your job, which was when I asked if I could bring it instead. I think he was glad to concede to that—he still harbours a small hope we'll see our way towards a match. I didn't like to tell him otherwise in case he said I couldn't come! But I suggested nothing, either, that might raise his hopes. I was very… noncommittal, I think is the right word to choose!'

Anton rolled his eyes and sighed. This day had been bound to happen. With the helicopter arriving, and Bea asking for him, his secret was out. He needed to speak to Lizzie before she heard this second-hand.

Now his concerns about his parents had been answered, Anton stepped forwards to embrace Beatrix in a hug, before standing back, his hands on her shoulders. He looked her up and down, pleasure on his face then leaned in again to kiss her soundly on both cheeks. 'I'm delighted to see you! You look well.'

He gave her a second, fervent hug, and realised that despite being happy here, he'd missed Bea, missed his home, even missed his stubborn papa.

'Here.' Beatrix delved into her shoulder bag and pulled out a long envelope, sealed with the royal coat of arms. 'You must read your letter. I was to give it into your hands immediately. You know what your father is like. Come, let's sit on the bench, and I will be patient. Then I'd love to see everything and meet Claire, too. Emily, I have met already, and she's lovely.'

'Lizzie. You must meet Lizzie, too.'

Anton didn't need to tell Beatrix more. She knew already Lizzie was special to him. 'I'm so pleased for you! But… what does she think of it all? I'm assuming you're coming back?'

'We'll see what my father has to say, but whatever it is, yes, I think I must. For a while, I imagined myself leaving for ever. Finding a job maybe more challenging than this, although as we're working on a massive restoration project, it's been quite full-on. But maybe not for life.' Anton led her by the hand to a bench, and they sat side by side, still talking earnestly. 'In the end, my sense of duty and also my love for Mondorra prevented this. I knew I'd come back one day. I hope with my father's blessing for the changes I want to put in place. But if not…' Anton shrugged and looked down at the letter he held in his hand.

Beatrix laid her hand on his arm. 'Open it.'

With nervous fingers, he tore the envelope open and pulled out a large, single sheet of heavy cream notepaper covered in his father's writing. A further pang of homesickness hit him. His parents had been good to him. His father was strict, but fair, albeit horribly old-fashioned and set in his ways. He was but a product of his own upbringing and so much had changed in his lifetime, it had to be bewildering for him. His mama was the loving parent, but also a loving wife, and often acted as a bridge between him and his father.

'*My son,*' Anton read. '*I hope this letter finds you well and contented. Helena tells me you are employed as a gardener and putting to good use all the tuition you have had from both her and Hansel. I am deeply glad that you chose to work as opposed to frittering away your time. It will have done you no harm to labour with your hands for a while, despite what I said about no prince of Mondorra working. Much better than idleness. That is another matter I was wrong about. Maybe this entire episode between us had been a testing time for us both?'*

Anton looked up with a smile. 'He's getting the occasional dig in.' But digs aside, this was a very promising beginning, and the knot of tension he'd carried for several months began to unravel and a lightness seeped into his body.

Beatrix threw back her head and laughed. 'But of course!'

Anton continued to read.

'Your mama and I were deeply saddened, however, that you left. For some while, I told myself we were well rid of you and your madcap ideas, while knowing all the time this was a lie. We love you, and we have missed you.'

Anton stopped reading again and closed his eyes. He'd missed them, too. A lot. Swallowing down a surge of emotion, he read on.

'I have discussed your plans for reform with various members of the government and have been shamed into the realisation you are right. We do indeed need to change our attitudes and approaches. Therefore, my dear son, I am writing to apologise, to concede defeat and to beg you to return. Not immediately, because you will have obligations to meet in your present employment, but as soon as you can. I hope you can find it in your heart to forgive a stubborn old man, and, in many ways, a frightened one. I was certain, should we change, the people might wish to end the monarchy, but I am told the opposite is more likely. If we do not *change,* then *the country might choose to rid itself of us.*

Which I really do not want, and interestingly, neither do the Mondorrans. The lynch pin is now you and whether you prefer to allow the monarchy to be dissolved, or return to your country and lead them into a more modern age, which I have been too slow to embrace.

I am, my dear Maximilian, your devoted papa, and your mama wishes for me to send her love.'

Sitting back on the bench, Anton let the letter dangle from his fingers, blinking the sudden sheen of tears from his eyes, which he could no longer prevent. Well, at least his father had come round, but such a shame they endured those months of argument and he'd had to leave to prove his point. Yet… if he hadn't, he wouldn't have met Lizzie.

'Read it.' He handed the letter to Beatrix.

'Well, good,' she said after reading it through and handing it back. 'That's good. So, you will come home?'

'Yes. Yes! The letter has made me very happy, and I'm glad we've broken through this horrible impasse and we can meet again as a family. But first, I *must* tell Lizzie. When we met earlier this summer, I told her I have a tough boss in my father, and a company which needs updating. It was all I could think of. I had feelings for her, but I wasn't sure how things would go and there seemed little point in pouring it all out then. Now, of course, we are in love and on Wednesday, she has to go back to London. I was going to spend today with her anyway, and explain everything.'

His initial reaction of joy to his father's letter began, slowly, to seep away, replaced by a cold dismay. The time had now come to find out if he had a future with Lizzie. Sweat broke out on his forehead, and he pressed his lips together, dread seeping into him at what was going to happen in the next few hours.

'But you still must! I'm sure someone else could show me round. Anton, you *must* explain to her and beg her to come to our country and at least look. It never crossed my mind she doesn't know who you are. Come.' She stood up and caught hold of his hand. 'Where is she? Take me to meet her, please?'

Anton glanced at his watch and immediately stood. 'It's late. She will have been back from her daily class for half an hour, and must be wondering where I am. She might be in the sitting-room, or maybe having a shower after class.'

Together, they ran up the steps and crossed the terrace. A scattering of dancers sat round with coffees and teas, reading papers, chatting. Of Lizzie, there was no sign.

In the reception hall, Sasha was on duty. He'd not had a lot to do with her, but she'd always been friendly and interested in the gardens.

'Good morning, Sasha.'

The receptionist looked from him to Bea, barely disguising her curiosity behind a professional manner.

'Anton… er, Anton? Or…?'

'Anton,' he replied firmly. 'I garden here, remember?'

Sasha dropped her eyes to the computer, a small smile twitching on her lips. 'Okay, Anton, if you say so. Can I help?'

'I'm looking for Lizzie. Is she in her room?'

'Lizzie's just gone out.'

'Oh. We were supposed to be meeting up. Any idea

where she went?'

'I don't, no. But Tim might? He was with her when they came out of the sitting-room and both went upstairs. She was looking pissed off, Anton. Sorry, but I think your friend was maybe the cause?'

'My frie—oh! Beatrix. Yes, I see.' He was silent for a few moments. 'Is Tim still here, or did he go with her?'

Looking up from her typing, Sasha nodded. 'Here, as far as I know. I'll ring his room. Go sit down and get some coffee. I'll send him through when he comes down.'

After several minutes, Tim Faversham came into the sitting-room, spotted them at a small table near the fireplace, and crossed to join them.

'As I think I said once before, you look familiar,' Tim said, as he sat down, speaking French. 'And I'm kind of putting two and two together here. You're not a UK national. Now we have a helicopter turning up and hey, I've met Lady Beatrix once, a long time ago. We were at a dinner together. So, Prince Maximilian, what's going on? Are you two an item?'

Anton looked stunned at Tim's very direct approach.

Beatrix had been staring at Tim ever since he entered the room, her eyes wide. Now, after he'd spoken, she leaned forwards, her voice eager. 'Yes, yes! I remember you. You were part of a theatre group. It was in Paris, yes?'

'Indeed it was. Maybe we can catch up later? Anyway, you asked me to join you, so you must have a reason.' Tim wasn't smiling. He eyed them both with severity.

'Why has Lizzie gone rushing off?' Anton sounded unhappy. 'And please, I am Anton here. Please?' His stomach churned, and he felt sick. Lizzie was upset. Where was she? He so needed to find her and explain everything.

Tim pursed his lips before speaking. 'Hmph. Okay, *Anton*. Lizzie rushed off because we finished class early. Because we came here to have a coffee before she went to find you. Because she saw you embracing Lady Beatrix and then sitting down side by side on the bench after you'd led her there by the hand, all of which looked very cosy. Minor reasons, perhaps, and maybe she should have waited and spoken to you, but I rather gather Bruno wasn't all he seemed, and she's a bit wobbly with relationships. So she said she wanted to go for a walk.'

'But how could she doubt me?'

'I'm not sure it was doubt so much as being unable to cope with complications and needing some thinking time? She said something about you wanting her to go to Mondorra, but was puzzled when you seemed on such friendly terms with Lady Beatrix. Look, I'm sure she'll be back soon, and you can sort it out. I'm taking that as a no to my question about you two being an item?' Tim's face was less frozen now. Warmth entered his eyes and a slight smile touched his lips as he looked from Anton to Beatrix, where he allowed his eyes to linger.

Bea picked up her coffee. 'Our parents wanted a match, but we're good friends and that's all we can ever be.'

'And here's another mystery.' Tim leaned forwards, forearms on his thighs, hands clasped in front of him. 'Why is the crown prince of Mondorra working as a humble gardener in a small corner of coastal Wales?'

Anton and Beatrix looked at each other warily before Anton answered. 'My papa wouldn't listen to the many proposals I put forward to modernise our country and I felt bored doing nothing. Now go to the damned newspapers, Tim—you'll probably get paid a good chunk of money by exposing me.'

'I wouldn't do that,' Tim said calmly.

Anton was taken aback, but also very relieved. 'Right. Good. Okay. Now look, is it okay if I leave you to look after Bea? Sorry, Bea, but I've got to find Lizzie and get things sorted out once and for all. I think I know where she might be, and I can't sit around and wait for her to come back.' He was far too on edge for that and needed action. He wanted an end to all this.

Without waiting for an answer, Anton strode from the room, eager to put everything to rights.

He had a letter stuffed into the back pocket of his jeans which was beckoning him back to a life of public duty, of being Crown Prince Maximilian, and one day, King Maximilian. If Lizzie refused to contemplate standing by his side, what then? Would duty win, or would he walk away from his country and hundreds of years of history for her sake? Other royals had done it—rarely, but they had—and lived a life in exile.

The choice was a bitter one… an impossible one.

All he could hope for was Lizzie loved him enough to at least try.

CHAPTER 15

Lizzie had got rid of some of her agitation by walking along the cliff. She'd felt annoyed and confused, returning to the hotel to see her lover embracing another woman. A very glamorous woman, at that, and one who seemed familiar, although Lizzie hadn't placed her as yet. How could Anton even think of doing something like that after what had happened between them last night? Anyway, who was this woman, and why was she so important she'd arrived by helicopter?

Although Anton had done much to dissipate the damage inflicted by Bruno, it seemed there was a small nugget of insecurity remaining, buried deep inside and of which she'd been unaware. But now, it was rearing up and trying to dominate her thoughts and cast doubt on Anton. Knowing him, she suspected there was a rational explanation for everything, but at this moment, she stomped along feeling thoroughly out of sorts.

Using her finger, she caught the tear which dribbled

down her cheek and wiped it on her jeans. Was she an old girlfriend? Unfinished business? But if the latter, why had Anton asked her to go with him to Mondorra? Why had he held off making love to her until she'd forced the issue last night? And what had he been going to say when she'd cut him off?

Maybe that he'd changed his mind? No! Everything she knew about Anton went against that. He wouldn't have then taken her to bed and made love to her if that's what he'd been about to say.

The path had risen revealing a small headland on her right. She turned off along a narrow track which broke away from the main path and led to its edge. There, she overlooked a rocky beach, with a small amount of sand on it, utterly deserted because it was inaccessible... unless you had a small boat, like those kayakers. Peering over the edge, she was completely unaware of anything, and when a voice spoke her name, she whirled round and stepped back, hardly able to believe who she saw.

Bruno!

A red mist rose in front of her eyes as she lashed out and caught him across his face, a slap intended for him, but also for Anton as well.

'What? *What?* Haven't you done enough to me? Why are you here? It *was* you I saw in Solhaven. Where have you been since then? Have you been stalking me?' Her words tumbled out, staccato in their fury, made worse by her anger with Anton. Her world was crashing down round her ears. Was it only this morning she'd woken in Anton's bed, warm and lazy from their love making?

And now this, faced with her biggest nightmare—Bruno intent on harming her! She flung her hands up in a gesture of fearful repudiation.

'*Lizzie!*' His voice was full of a terror she couldn't understand, and shock widened his eyes. His hand reached out as he stepped forwards.

Her legs became weak, and her arms came up to curl round her head.

This was the moment she'd always feared.

He would push her over the cliff, and even if she survived, she'd probably never dance again.

His hand grasped her arm, and he pulled her strongly towards him as she teetered on the cliff's edge.

Pulled her?

Not pushed?

Pulled her to safety, yes, and now held her in the circle of his arms, looking at her in concern. '*Fuck*, Lizzie! You scared me half to death then! Do you realise how close you were to that edge? One tiny step back and you'd have lost your footing! I didn't mean to startle you like that, but I was walking back to Solhaven, and as I came round the corner, I saw you here, and—oof!'

From nowhere, two men appeared each side of Bruno and caught him by his arms, jerking him backwards so he fell on the ground.

He looked startled, his eyes wide, his mouth slack-jawed. 'Who the *hell* are you? What do you think you're doing? I know this lady. I just wanted to… needed to…' he twisted in their grip, trying to stand upright. 'Lizzie! Tell them we know each other! Tell them to let me go!'

Lizzie turned away, intending to return to the hotel, throw herself on her bed and have a damned good cry. This was all too much. First Anton and that woman, now Bruno! She was afraid of him; she thought he would take this opportunity to destroy her newly found confidence again, and she couldn't—she halted and turned slowly back.

'Bruno?'

The two men still hung onto him, faces grimly set with tight mouths and narrowed eyes. Who the hell were they? Surely not passing Good Samaritans?

'Bruno?' Lizzie asked again, her voice tentative.

For Bruno had spoken clearly. He hadn't sworn or made any threats. His skin was a good colour. His eyes were once again the clear blue she remembered from their early days.

And he'd saved her from possibly falling backwards over that cliff edge.

'Please tell them to let me go,' Bruno begged from his ignominious position on the ground, shame in his eyes. 'I don't mean you any harm, Lizzie. I… need to say a few things to you, I promise that's all.'

Lizzie looked at the men, her eyebrows raised. 'I think you can release him.'

'We understood he was a danger to you.' The man who spoke had an accent.

Lizzie's eyes widened even further. 'Who told you that?'

They looked at each other, and one of them shook his head slightly. 'We can't say.'

'But…' Lizzie looked bewildered. 'But… how did you know he was here in Solhaven?'

Again, that exchanged look between the two men. 'We were asked to make sure you were safe if you left the hotel or your dancing group.'

Lizzie's breath hissed out. The only people she'd told about maybe seeing Bruno had been Tim and Anton. The only one who knew how afraid she'd been of her ex-partner was Anton. So was he responsible for this? Did it make her angry or grateful? Ah, she could think about all that later.

'Let him go. Now. Once, he might have been a danger to me, but not any longer. Let him go and leave us alone.'

Slowly and reluctantly the two men released Bruno's arms and faded away, but they didn't actually leave—just stood several yards away. If they hadn't tackled Bruno, she would have taken no notice of them; in their tee shirts, shorts, and trainers they looked like a couple of holiday makers.

'I'm sorry about that,' Lizzie turned from watching them and spread her hands, her face thoughtful. Who *was* Anton, if indeed it had been him who'd organised bodyguards? Bodyguards, private helicopters, a ritzy-looking woman he rushed to greet, a large firm in Mondorra, which needed modernising… but of which she'd found no mention when she'd searched the internet a couple of weeks ago. Quite the opposite, in fact. The articles she'd found suggested the country was sadly lagging behind its European neighbours, and there were no big companies.... Shrugging, she brought her attention back to Bruno.

He scrabbled upright. 'It's all right. Honestly, I can understand someone wanted to look after you. They must know what happened before, and they wanted to make sure you were safe. On Saturday, I-I couldn't believe it when I saw the poster, that it was you who'd be dancing at the school. I couldn't believe it. Then I thought it would be so good if I could see you, to speak to you and—'

'But what are you *doing* here? Come, let's walk back to the beach, if that's where you were heading.'

They turned and walked side by side. A quick glance over her shoulder told her the two men had fallen behind, too far away to hear their conversation, but no doubt close enough to reach her if there was a problem. She was more than confident there wouldn't be.

'I thought I'd seen you a couple weeks ago, in Solhaven one morning, when our bus went through. I was frightened. I thought you'd come to harm me.'

He looked at his feet in silence. When he finally raised his head, his eyes shone with tears. 'I'm so ashamed, Lizzie. So, so ashamed of what happened. I've been down here almost ever since the company kicked me out. I went on a binge that same week, and I ended up being beaten up. I woke up in a gutter, covered in blood and my own vomit.'

She flinched.

He sighed. 'Someone visited me in hospital. You'll laugh when I tell you it was a vicar, and she talked to me a lot. Of my parents, of you—I told her who I was—of my own life and what would happen if I continued down this road. She made me think. She helped me get into a rehab place. It's about ten miles inland from here.'

Lizzie shot him a look, her eyes widening as her hand came up to cover her mouth. *'Rehab?* Here?'

'Yeah. Ironic isn't it, that we both ended up in nearly the same place? Anyway, they didn't let me out for a long time and then it was only occasionally, for a trip to the beach somewhere. Eventually, I was trusted with the town—that's probably when you saw me. I'd no idea the outreach was here until I saw that poster advertising your last performance. It was enough of a surprise it was the MetroCapital outreach, but you can imagine my utter shock when I saw your name as the leading dancer. I desperately wanted to watch, so I bought a ticket. You danced brilliantly. I was so proud of you.'

Lizzie's stride faltered. This was Bruno as she'd first known him. This was the Bruno she'd thought herself in love with, and indeed, still held him in affection, *as he was now*. However, there was an element of distrust that ran through her, and she knew she'd never be in love with him again, never wanted to recreate their partnership. He'd done her too much harm ever to go back. She hoped that wasn't why he wanted to talk.

'I'm sorry.' Bruno walked beside her, but left a good foot of space between them. 'This must be a shock, and I can understand those goons tackling me when I approached you. I admit to asking around and finding out where you were staying. I came along the beach from Solhaven, and I was trying to pluck up the courage to come up to the hotel and ask to speak to you. I couldn't, so I walked out here along the cliffs to see if I could manage any better when I returned. Then, coming back, I saw you right in front of me.'

Lizzie sent him a sideways look from under her lashes. 'What were you going to say, if you'd come to the hotel?'

He spoke with simple sincerity. 'That I'm sorry. Bitterly sorry for everything. I've had quite a lot of input from this place and realised I was frightened at how high I'd flown, and I didn't think I could keep it up. The drink helped, but then I moved onto coke, and it was such a fucking mistake. I became obnoxious and dangerous, but I don't expect you to forgive me because I don't deserve it. I never intended to sink so low that I harmed you, or to make those revolting threats. I know you and I will never dance together again. I wanted to tell you I'm going back to South Africa, and I've been offered a place as the ballet master of a biggish company there. I really think I'll be happy passing on what I know.' Fingers twisting together, Bruno's torrent of words finally ended.

Lizzie inhaled a slow breath as her whole body released a tension she'd not been aware of until she heard Bruno's words. A warmth filled her, which started in her heart and gently seeped through her. She stopped, swallowed, and threw back her head, eyes closed, as she suppressed her tears. She was glad the last remnants of the cloud hovering above her had disappeared and was truly happy Bruno had found his way back from the living hell into which he'd fallen. Straightening, she sniffed and wiped her hands over her face, accepting the clean tissue Bruno silently held out to her. 'Thanks. Thank you.'

They walked on and descended the path onto the beach. Lizzie stopped by a rock and turned to face him. 'What now?'

'I'm not staying to chat.' Bruno shifted from foot to foot. 'I just needed to say how sorry I am and let you know I'm leaving the country. I wish you all the best. Your new partner seems very good.'

Lizzie laid her hand on his arm. 'I'm so pleased for you. I'm thankful you've kicked the habits and delighted you've found a job that suits you. You'll be a brilliant ballet master, you know.'

There were a few moments of silence as they held each other's gaze. Then Lizzie stepped forwards and hugged him, kissing his cheek. 'Go forward, my friend, and if you really want to show me how sorry you are, don't you ever drink or take coke again, okay?'

Bruno gave a shaky laugh and stepped back from her embrace. 'I never intend to, that I can promise.'

'You said you could never ask for my forgiveness, but I'm giving it to you.'

At her words, Bruno turned away abruptly and pressed his forefinger and thumb over his closed eyelids. 'Thank you. God, thank you. I'm going now. Good luck, Lizzie. Fly high. Fly free.'

Turning on his heel, he set off at a jog over the hard-packed sand, a hand lifted to his face as he wiped away tears, just as she was doing. Through her own tears, his form blurred and wavered as it receded in the distance, and she slowly lowered herself to the rock.

'Oh!' Startled, she raised her head.

Fly high. Fly free!

Those flowers had come from Bruno! A farewell. A benediction. And his words today had indeed enabled her to fly high and fly free.

CHAPTER 16

Anton was certain Lizzie would have gone to the beach. They'd spent many happy hours walking on the sands or the cliff paths, and she loved it, found the incessant waves soothing. He was going to talk to her, beg her to at least consider staying with him, to see what happened and how things might progress, to find solutions to the major obstacles in their way. Anton swallowed. Major obstacles? Asking her to sign up to be the crown princess? Of course, it would be nothing like this country's royalty. But once many of his own reforms were in place, he was hoping for something more like other European countries had—working royals. Royals on bicycles. Royals who were part of their country's life and not rare exhibits in a goldfish bowl.

He scooped back his hair and stood, surveying the beach below him. There she was, sitting on a rock.

"Max!"

Turning, he saw Bea running towards him, consternation on her face, her phone in her hand. He patted his pockets and remembered he'd left his phone on the small table next to his bed. He'd wanted no interruptions.

What was the matter? What was wrong? Why did Bea look so worried?

Panting, she skidded to a stop next to him and held out the phone as she tried to catch her breath. He took it, held it to his ear. It was his father.

'Put it on speaker,' Beatrix hissed.

Flashing her a questioning look, Anton complied.

'Maximilian, my son. Have your read my letter?'

'I have,' he replied, glancing at Bea and raising his eyebrows, shock lancing through him. He was being swept from Lizzie back to Mondorra. Happiness at being back in contact with his father and having made his point about the country warred with anguish about Lizzie, and his worry concerning her reaction to what he needed to tell her.

'I wish again to apologise to you.'

'Papa, no. You've said it all in your letter. It's behind us, and we can move on. Is that why you called? To make sure I'd seen the letter?'

'Partly, partly, yes. But... your mama and I have missed you, and as I said in my letter, I'm sure you'll have to finish what you are doing at this hotel before you can come home. As it might yet be some time until we see you, I have a plan. We must come to England in a few days' time, anyway, for the wedding of the king's niece. We thought... we thought maybe we could come to the hotel first and see where you have been living and working? Beatrix tells us the hotel is very pleasant and quite small. It seems there is a suite of rooms which are fortuitously free, and we thought we could be—how do you say it—under the radar? Your mama especially would like to see where you have been all this time. And we could discuss when you might come back?'

Now not only had Anton's eyebrows risen, but his eyes were open wide and his jaw had dropped. He looked round wildly, at Bea, at the beach where Lizzie perched on her rock, back up to the hotel and swallowed. 'Mmm, ye-yes. Are you sure the rooms are free, though? This place is very busy, and I'm surprised.'

'They are only free for two nights, so we are lucky. We can arrive by tomorrow evening. My son, I shall be delighted to see you.'

The call ended. Numbly, Anton returned the phone to Bea and looked at her, his hands spread at his sides, an expression of anguish on his face.

'*Fuck*. It's all falling to pieces. I suppose you checked the rooms?'

'I'm sorry, Max. They asked me to see what the hotel was like and what type of rooms might be available, yes. I didn't realise they planned to come so soon. I'd forgotten about the wedding. They must have contacted the hotel since I called to let them know what the place was like.'

'But what about staff?'

Bea shrugged. 'I don't know. Maybe there are some other rooms available, or somewhere else they can stay and be driven here early in the morning. They knew you'd already requested a security detail, but until I told them where you were, that was all.'

'Did they know why I wanted my men?'

'No. No, they know nothing about Lizzie.'

Anton stood silent, his eyes finding his feet an object of fascination, before raising his head and letting his breath hiss out through clenched teeth, a frown narrowing his eyes as he looked down at the beach. 'I must talk to Lizzie. I must try to explain. Go back to Tim. Get him to show you round. Tell you what, I'm very proud of my vegetables in the walled garden. Tell him to take you to have a look at them.'

Bea snorted with laughter. 'Vegetables? Seriously?'

'Not seriously, but it seems to fit in with this farce fast developing around us.'

'Okay, why not? Max, Anton, whatever you want to call yourself—it'll all work out, honestly.'

'What? With Lizzie? Asking her to marry me—you know we can't live together—and expecting her to be crown princess, just like that? You think she'll accept it and fall into my arms?'

'If she really loves you,' Bea said reassuringly. 'If she really loves you, she'll find a way through, a way to manage. After all, what's so different between having hundreds of people watch you on stage, or hundreds of people watch you while you cut a ribbon for a new hospital?'

'Ah, but you forget—she has a career to follow, and I cannot expect her just to drop it. You've seen her dance. You know how good she is. So it's not just facing crowds, is it? It's like asking me to walk away from my path in life, if I ask her to stop dancing.'

'Ah. Yes, of course. Oh, damn, why are decisions so hard?'

Bea walked back towards the hotel, and Anton watched her, a thoughtful look on his face as he considered her comment. Indeed, what was so different? It was all performing, in a way. Maybe Lizzie would accept this after all? His stomach churned. The coffee he'd drunk sat there uneasily. What a mess, and of his own making, he knew that, but he thought he'd have time. Bea turning up and now his parents descending on Haven House was not what he'd expected.

He resumed his walk down to the beach, slower now, postponing when he had to admit the firm was Mondorra itself, and his job was not vice president or whatever she'd assumed he did, but crown prince. He'd tasted freedom as a student and again for the last few months. Being royalty wasn't as glamorous or easy as people thought. You were tied down to duty and protocol. Yet… once his reforms were in place, there would be greater freedom for himself and his wife. A chance to spend much of their lives living fairly normally, although obviously there would be engagements, banquets, entertaining foreign dignitaries. His mind kept returning to the idea she could set up a ballet school, too. Maybe a company…

He stopped, turned and stared back at the hotel. Bea! Bea and Tim Faversham, who spoke fluent French. If those two took up together, Tim might also live in Mondorra and he and Lizzie could dance…

He shook his head. What an imagination. Wishful thinking.

Lizzie was still sitting on the rock. Perhaps the same one where they'd talked on the very first evening Lizzie had arrived in Wales, although there was a cluster of several, all close to each other. He approached slowly, and he didn't speak until he was near.

'Lizzie.' He knew he sounded tired, and probably worried as well.

'This is turning into a strange day,' Lizzie said, turning to look at him, apparently unsurprised to find him there. 'This morning, when I woke up after our glorious night, there was nothing in front of me other than a morning class and spending the rest of the day with you.'

Anton moved closer and indicated the space next to her, relieved when she gave a silent consent by shifting slightly over to one side to create more room. Sitting side by side, his shoulder touched hers, and his thigh felt her warmth. It soothed him and for several moments they sat regarding the water, hearing the hush of waves and the evocative cries of the gulls which always told you stories of the sea, so even inland, it was possible to envisage the wide expanse of water, timeless and enduring.

'Who is the woman I saw you embracing?' Lizzie still stared ahead when she spoke, her voice low. 'Should I be concerned? I admit to feeling some jealousy.'

'No need for concern or jealousy, that I promise. Bea —Beatrix—is someone I have known since I was a small. We grew up together, and we're like brother and sister. Our parents hoped for a match, but we both knew it could never be.'

Lizzie remained silent as she considered his words, then she gave a nod. 'Okay. Why is she here?'

'To give me a letter. A very important letter.'

'Did she come in that helicopter? We saw it on the grass as we came down the drive.'

'She did.'

'Your boss? Your father, I think you said? The one who won't modernise? You also said you hoped one day he would realise it was needed and would ask you to go back. Is that what the letter was about?'

He slid his fingers through hers, entwined them, held on tight. 'It was.'

'He's got a great deal of control over your life, it seems. Planning a dynastic marriage and not allowing you any say in this company of yours you keep talking about.'

'Yes. But he's also very loving.'

He heard Lizzie sigh before she leaned her head against his shoulder. 'I assume it was you who arranged two guys to monitor me?'

Jerking upright, snatching his fingers from hers, Anton took her face between his hands and turned her head so he could look at her. 'Strange question. Why? What happened? Yes, it was me, but there's no way you should have known unless... *Bruno*! Has Bruno tried to do something? Harm you?'

'Calm down.' She caught hold of his wrists and pulled his hands down. 'Yes, Bruno. But not what you think. That's one thing I was thinking of, when I said this day hadn't unwound the way I expected.'

'Tell me.' He looked round, saw two men some distance away, sitting on the sand and leaning back against a rock. To anyone else, they'd appear to be idle holiday makers, but Anton recognised them as being from the palace security team. *'Tell* me. What happened? If he's hurt you, I swear, I'll—'

'Calm down. How could he hurt me, seeing those two guys were shadowing every move?' She laid her hand on his thigh and nodded in their direction, a small smile curving her lips. 'Bruno bumped into me on the cliff path. Apparently he's been down here for a few months, in a rehab place about ten miles away, he said. He startled me and I nearly fell backwards over the edge of the cliffs, but he saved me. He grabbed my arm and pulled me away.'

Lizzie then told him about Bruno's recovery, his remorse and his future plans.

Anton listened carefully, a deep relief flooding him that the spectre of Bruno would no longer cast long shadows over her life. 'You're happy, aren't you? Really happy?'

Wonder filled his voice, his eyes softened, and his own mouth echoed her happiness with a gentle smile. Despite what Bruno had done, she'd forgiven him. His heart burst with love for her generosity of spirit.

'I am.'

She sat in a tranquil silence for a few moments then shifted, turning so she could look fully into his face, her eyes narrowed.

His stomach curdled with dread.

'Let's get back to you, shall we? How do you have the wherewithal to employ two men to hang around doing nothing very much, in case someone I might have seen tried to harm me? And how come your father can afford to send a helicopter to deliver a letter? Your boss. The *firm*. Have I fallen in love with a member of the Mafia? It seems so ridiculous to even think that, but...' She shrugged.

Anton's dread briefly gave way to a shout of laughter as he threw back his head in amusement. 'No. Not Mafia.'

He sobered rapidly and looked at her, his head tilted, his eyes serious. 'But... maybe I haven't been as truthful as I could have been. It's true my father is above me, and he didn't want to modernise and change things the way I wanted to. It was for those reasons I left. All of that is true. And you're right, he's written to me and agreed to reform, so we can be much more modern, and there will be less of a burden on him if I go back and work alongside. And yes, it is true he also wanted me to marry Bea, but she and I knew that could never happen.'

'So, tell me about this company of which there's no trace on the internet? In fact, what I found is that Mondorra is falling behind, and needs modernising and...' Her voice trailed away and she looked at him, her eyes narrowed. 'What, exactly, *is* your job?'

'Yes, we are now at the critical moment. I'm so afraid you'll listen to what I'm going to say and shake your head. I beg you. I *beg* you to think it over and consider everything. Bea said something wise just before I came down here.' His words tumbled from his mouth, and he gripped one of her hands far too tightly. Sweat beaded on his forehead.

Sliding off the rock he paced forwards a short way, stopped and wheeled round to face her.

'What did Bea say?'

'That you danced in front of hundreds of people and were watched and admired by them. That it was only a slight difference to what you would do by my side if you agreed… if you agreed to marry me.'

'*Marry* you? Last I heard it was if I'd *go* to Mondorra with you, and I don't think I ever answered because we had other things on our minds, if you remember?'

His face softened, and he smiled. 'Oh, I remember. Every little detail.'

'Yes, well, perhaps we shouldn't start getting distracted. We should concentrate on the here and now.'

He loved the blush that ran across her cheekbones. 'If you say so, but maybe we *should* think about last night? It's obvious we love each other very much, I think.'

'Look, you've said a lot of confusing things, and much as I'd like to make love again, we need to sort things out, and why you've jumped from just going to Mondorra to getting married.'

'Go to Mondorra, first. Look round. Get an idea of what you might be doing. Bea can help you there. But one day, we'd have to get married.'

'Have to?' He saw her lip curl as she looked at him dubiously.

'I'm putting this all the wrong way. I want to be with

you. I love you. I'd like be with you forever because I think I could face anything with you by my side. But we would, one day, need to marry.'

'Anton, you're avoiding the answer again. Spit it out, will you?' Lizzie jumped down from the rock and stood face to face with him, one eyebrow raised, her head tilted to one side. Stepping forwards, she took both his hands in hers, and a warmth flooded through him at her simple gesture.

'Oh, Lizzie. I'm not a gardener—'

'I think I've already guessed that!'

Anton wrapped his arms round her, pulling her close and resting his cheek on her hair. 'I love you. I'm so afraid of losing you. My future would be bearable if I had you by my side.'

Lizzie drew back and frowned at him. 'Tell me, and we'll finally know if you're going to lose me or not.'

He flinched, a jolt which ran from his head down to his feet, and he saw the surprise on her face.

'What?' she asked slowly, serious now. '*What?*'

'You remember the royal reception, meeting the king and queen, that night we spoke for the first time?'

'Yes?'

'They are my parents.'

There was a long silence. Lizzie stepped back from his embrace, and dread seeped into him like a black miasma coiling through every part of his body. He staggered and caught hold of the rock to keep himself upright. This, then, was it. The end. His swan princess would fly away, and he'd be left facing an utterly bleak future.

'I wish it needn't be so. I've considered throwing it all up, I truly have. But... but I can't! I can't just walk away from my country,' he finished sadly, as tears blinded him. He turned from her and dashed a hand over his eyes.

He heard her suck in a deep breath and tensed, waiting for the words he was so sure would come. There was silence. When he turned, Lizzie had her back turned to him and was staring at the sea, that eternally shifting mass of water which soothed, saddened or exhilarated, depending on its mood.

'Lizzie? Please, *say* something! If it's to be no, then tell me quickly. I can't bear much more of this. I've been worrying about it ever since we met again. I knew almost immediately I loved you. But this, being the crown princess, it's a heavy burden for you and—'

She held up her hand. 'Give me a moment, okay? Just... give me a moment?'

She walked towards the sea, her arms tight round her body. Anton couldn't see her face and didn't know how she was reacting. Within a few seconds, though, she'd turned and marched off along the edge of the water, gradually getting smaller as she determinedly walked away from him.

So that was it? Slumping against the rock, Anton bowed his head and covered his eyes. An occasional tear escaped to make silver tracks down his cheeks. He'd been so certain if she said no he'd be able to face his future without her. Now, despite his brave words, he didn't think he could.

He slid down until he sat on the sand, his back

against the rough stone, his head tipped up towards the sun, eyes closed, as his heart slowly fell apart, and he stayed motionless for a very long time.

The two bodyguards eventually approached.

'Your highness—'

'Go away!'

'But—'

'*Go away!*'

Eventually, the incoming tide splashed cold, salty water over his feet, rushed in, filled the hollow around the rock, soaked him entirely. He dragged himself upright.

Maybe he *would* have to leave his country after all? It would break his heart, but it broke his heart even more to lose Lizzie. Which heartbreak would be the worst? He gripped his hair on each side of his head to still the pounding thoughts. Now the chance to make a difference in his country was within reach, he would truly suffer if he walked away. He honestly didn't think he could, but *if* he did—just consider *if* he did—he thought he might end up losing respect for himself, his purpose in life, the needs of his country.

He had to go back.

But... a future without Lizzie was bleak indeed.

Oh, where *was* she?

He moved sluggishly to the steps leading to the cottage. He had the right to sit on them, because this was soon to be his new lodgings. Resting his forearms on his thighs, he dropped his face into his hands.

Lizzie. Where had she gone? To Bruno, maybe? Back, somehow, to the hotel?

The tide came fully in. The waves broke only two or three feet away from his perch. Hours must have passed. Somehow, he must find the strength to get up and drag himself up to the hotel, beg Tim to find Lizzie, and tell her he had to talk to her.

And then what?

Hope she would come to him and listen.

It was all he could do.

Despite the warmth of the late summer afternoon, Anton shivered. Shock, and his wet clothes, as well as no food since his very early breakfast were all contributing to his misery. He rubbed his hands down his face, and staggered to his feet, to turn and go up the steps and to his room in the hostel.

'Anton?'

Lizzie!

He stopped, motionless, one hand reaching for the small gate in front of him to support his leaden body, which braced for the blow he knew must come.

Finding hidden strength, he whirled to face her. '*Lizzie*. I've been thinking so much since you left. I want you in my life so much, but you have the right to continue to dance, too. Yet Mondorra needs me to lead them. so I have to go. Please tell me you will understand this? I've considered leaving my country, but I truly think I would hate myself and this would affect us, so in the end, both relationships would be damaged beyond repair. I think I have to give you up, my beloved. To give you your freedom. I think…' He buried his face in his hands and wept.

She stared at him, her eyes wide, her hand coming

up to cover her mouth as tears sprang into her eyes. 'What?' It was a whispered word he hardly heard, but sensed.

'I wish I could give Mondorra up, I really do. I've spent all afternoon since you left, thinking it all over, from every angle. Agonising about it. Maybe you would dance some more out there in the world and come to me when you can? Maybe one day you will want to stop. Then you can come to Mondorra, and I will build you a ballet school.' He ached for his empty life but it was no good. He couldn't walk away from what needed doing.

She moved closer and looked up at him. 'You'd do that, for *me*?' Her voice was full of incredulity. 'Build a ballet school?'

'Yes!'

'Oh, *Anton*.'

He ached to pull her into his arms, bury his face in her hair, weep on her shoulder as she'd wept on his, but now wasn't the moment to give way. 'One day, for when you finish your dancing on stage. Yes, it can be done and Mondorra would benefit.'

'Thank you!' Her eyes shone, her mouth parted. 'It's always been a dream of mine, to start a school, but a pipe dream, for how could I afford to do something like that?'

While he was glad he'd made her happy, inside his heart was breaking for another reason. He didn't know when she'd be ready to walk away from the international stage and be with him. Would it be enough if she agreed to join him sometime in the future? Ah, hell! It would have to be. Better than not at all. And he would just have to be patient and wait and trust in her love for him, take the crumbs she offered. So many times he'd been tempted to choose her above his country, but he knew it couldn't be done.

After a few moments, Lizzie started to talk again. 'I walked into Solhaven and had a coffee. I didn't expect you'd still be here when I came back. I had to come via the cliff path because the tide's in, but the walk did me good. You've let yourself get soaked!'

'I lost track of time,' Anton mumbled.

'I can't tell you how wonderful you are, being prepared to fulfill my lifelong dream. It touches me beyond all imagining, and I thank you from the bottom of my heart.'

Fuck! This sounded as if a refusal was coming. He braced himself for the blow.

'I did a lot of thinking, too. I know you can't leave your country, for you wouldn't be the man of principle I love if you did. I also decided you've let this grow out of all proportion and turned it into a monster.' She came up the steps and took hold of his icy hands. 'It isn't a monster, my love. Mondorra is small, isn't it? You want to modernise it, which I assume will remove a lot of pomp from your role. And Bea is right. I presume I'll have to do stuff occasionally and be in the papers and dress up, but she said it was little different to being on stage, and she's *right*. It's simple, you see—I can't be without you, and I'm not prepared for you to lose everything for my sake. Over these last few weeks, I've learned I like you, have fun with you, physically lust for you, and when you combine all of that, it turns into love. I *love* you, Anton. I love you with all my heart. I can't say the idea of being a princess thrills me because when I go home after a performance, I can close my door, kick of my shoes and just chill—'

'You still can!' He almost shouted in his relief, his disbelief. Joy welled up and spilled through him, turning his legs to water. His hands trembled as he clasped hers. His love, his swan princess. 'Truly, you would do this for me? But your dancing?'

She gently shook her head, her hair blowing in the breeze that had come up from nowhere, the afternoon rapidly cooling. 'I can dance. I wanted to dance again, like I did before, and prove Bruno hadn't taken that from me, and I've already done that. Now he's apologised and explained, and I know he's recovered, it's even better. Maybe another year on the international stage? We can meet in that time, surely? This is the modern world and after all—' Her voice broke, and tears came into her eyes. 'All you need to do is snap your fingers and hey, a helicopter will take you where you want.'

'We have a jet, too,' he murmured softly, a glint of humour entering his eyes for the first time in hours.

'These are all things we can sort out. Once I've had my chance to regain my place in the ballet world, then I'll take your ballet school.' Lizzie smiled, then paused before continuing in a soft voice. 'But, and very much more importantly, I'll take *you*, my love. Kiss me, Anton. Hold me and kiss me. Please?'

Still trembling from her acceptance of who he was,

and her utter generosity in accepting his terms, he pulled her into his arms and slowly lowered his mouth to her lips, touching them, parting them with his tongue, his hands splayed on her buttocks even as hers locked round his neck.

His kiss deepened, his tongue seeking further access as his body hardened and she pushed against him, her breathing becoming rapid, her hands tangled in his hair.

'Come back to my room?' he asked hoarsely.

Words, just minutes ago, he'd thought never to say again.

CHAPTER 17

THEY WOKE EARLY the following morning, Anton and Lizzie, after secreting themselves in his room for the rest of yesterday. Both had turned off their phones after each sending a text, his to Bea, hers to Tim. They'd made love and talked. He'd heated small items of food in the microwave and made endless cups of coffee as they discussed how they should move forwards. They'd further discussed the idea of the ballet school and possibly a company, too, and wondered if Tim would be interested in joining the scheme. So much to talk about. So much to consider.

Now it was nearly sunrise.

They looked at each other with the growing realisation that they would have to emerge. There was going to be a lot of explaining. During the night spent talking, making love and sleeping, they'd settled some basic points.

Anton had to work, at least for this morning. If his father wanted him to come back immediately, he was going to suggest a palace gardener came over until Claire could find his replacement.

Lizzie had to speak to William, and also to Harry, the director, and Peter, the senior ballet master, to find out their plans for her, and then she and Anton would talk some more. She knew she was due some holiday, and it was most unlikely she was wanted for the winter season because they would already have cast those ballets. Anton's suggestion of starting a ballet school, and maybe even a company, in Mondorra had stunned her. She intended to ask Tim if he'd be happy to help found it. He'd mentioned returning to France at some point, and Mondorra was bordered by France. She even wondered whether MetroCapital would like to be part of it. Ideas raced through her head. It was hard to believe her long-held dreams might—no, *would*—become a reality.

They both planned to ask Jake, Emily, Claire, Daniel, Tim and Bea for lunch, to tell them what was going on, and they arranged for the coach to come and collect the rest of the ballet company, take them to Silver Sands and pay for their lunches at the café, so the dining-room would be free of their curious eyes.

'Tell Tim he can stay on a few days and have a lift back to London with my parents. Bea mentioned two nights and they must be in London soon, anyway, because they must attend a wedding. Tim might enjoy a bit of holiday, especially if Bea is here, too. Now—I am starting work very early today. I will need to clean up and look tidy for our lunch, and I won't be able to work this afternoon because I don't know when my parents will arrive. Can I leave you to set up the lunch and see if Tim wants to stay? He can look after Bea.' Anton grinned before turning back to the mirror to brush his hair.

Lizzie gazed at him, her love swamping her, as he sagged at the knee to look in the mirror. She laughed as he promptly ran the fingers of both hands through his hair as soon as he'd put the brush down and undid all his good work. The future was daunting, but she was sure she'd be able to manage. She believed Anton's reassurances they would have much private time together.

'What *is* your title?' she asked now, a little nervously.

He directed a sharp look at her, his eyes narrowing as he obviously heard the tremor in her voice.

He sat on the edge of the bed, brushing her hair back from her face with gentle fingers. 'Crown Prince Maximilian. If you want all my names, then Maximilian Alessandro Anton de Casimir, of Mondorra.'

'And me?'

'Crown princess Lizzie.'

'That sounds silly.' Lizzie lay back on her pillows and pouted, folding her arms.

'Are you Elizabeth?'

'No. I'm plain Eliza.'

'Then Crown Princess Eliza.'

Lizzie covered her face with her hands before dragging them down and expelling a long breath as she shook her head. 'It still sounds silly. Yes, yes, stop looking so worried. I said I'd do it. I can do it. But… just get your modernisation over and done with as fast as you can, okay?'

She saw him look away, sadness compressing his mouth.

'What?'

'I can't rush them,' he said, his voice muffled. 'I will need to be careful. Can you be patient, my swan princess?'

He leaned forwards, his lips touching hers, and even that softly gentle kiss had her stomach lurching. Brushing her hand over the zip of his jeans, she looked up at him and saw the answering passion on his face before he straightened and gave her a mock stern look.

'Enough. Later.'

'Wait! Wait! Let me throw something on. I'll come with you out into the garden, and we can see the sun rise, then I'll come back and shower.'

Within minutes she was ready, and they walked into the garden where the sky had lightened from dark to mid-blue, a few stars still visible. Apart from the distant, soft sound of the waves, there was a complete hush, even the seagulls were quiet. Heavy dew made the grass look grey in the half-light, but every minute the sky lightened, and when the first rays of the sun broke over the fields behind the old house, the greyish hue of the grass changed and became lushly green with a veil of delicate silver thrown over. Looking back on the lawn, they could see their footprints where they'd walked through the dew-heavy grass. The slight chill in the air dispersed as the sun rose higher, and the perfume of flowers floated up from the roses, the borders, and the mixed flower beds along the old walls of the kitchen gardens. And then the morning chorus broke the silence—blackbirds, a thrush, various unidentifiable birds with pretty chirrups and in the distance, some larks.

For a moment, they stood absolutely still as the miracle of morning and sunrise overwhelmed them, both taking deep breaths to appreciate the surrounding scents.

'It's so beautiful,' Lizzie whispered. 'So, so beautiful.' Then she smiled and reached up to kiss Anton. 'But I have things to do, as well as you. I'll see you at lunchtime.'

Their gathering took place in the hotel dining-room. It was often quiet at lunchtimes because the guests had taken themselves off to explore or had taken the hotel's picnic lunch offer, or would eat out, and the ballet company had been delighted about their outing and had all happily trooped off.

Lizzie arrived before Anton, and the murmured conversations died down as she walked over and sat in one of the two remaining places. She smiled nervously at Tim, the only person she really knew well in the group. One lunch with Claire and Daniel didn't really count, and she'd only seen Emily and Jake in passing. Bea, she'd not met at all.

Conversation gradually re-started, but she was aware of the looks coming her way. Not unfriendly— no, not at all. Just… curious. Very curious. She wished Anton would hurry.

Tim patted her hand. 'Well, even I don't know what's

going on, although I rather gather you've caught yourself a real, live prince.'

'Shhh.' Lizzie looked round the table, but no-one was listening. She nodded towards Bea, seated on his other side, chatting to Emily. 'Did you know Bea before?'

'I met her, a couple of years ago. We… got on rather well together, but she was on an official visit and was whisked away before we could get to know each other better. It's good to see her again.' He gave a small smile, and his eyes glowed.

'I'm glad. I hope things go the way you both want.'

Heads turned. Anton strode across the dining-room with a pleasant smile and, pulling out his chair, he sat. 'Thank you for agreeing to meet with Lizzie and me this lunchtime.' He looked round and caught everyone's eye.

Lizzie's eyebrows rose. This was a new side of Anton and clearly the result of his position.

'Yeah, right,' Jake said, lounging back in his chair. 'I don't mind a bit of time off. Jenny took over for me. But if you don't mind me saying, this is weird. I mean, we know you and Lizzie here have started a relationship, and that's great… but why do we need to be told? If you want a wedding held here, cool. Emily's the one to ask about that.'

Lizzie was amused. In his own casual way, Jake could control the meeting just as ably as Anton. She had a vision of this gorgeous hunk with his blonde curls bent over a bath with a tiny surfboard and his baby, and grinned.

'It's nice to have a lunchtime off,' Emily said

peaceably. 'Annie's enjoying herself upstairs with Olivia and Jamie all to herself and I'm enjoying myself here, with a glass of wine and relaxing.'

Anton placed his hands on the table and sighed. 'You have guests arriving sometime this afternoon.'

Emily and Jake exchanged cautious glances then looked at Bea, who simply smiled.

'We have,' Emily conceded. 'And if Lady Beatrix is also a guest at this lunch, I'm wondering about links here.'

'We always called you the mysterious gardener,' Jake interjected with a grin.

'He knows a lot about art,' Claire added. 'He knows Daniel's work.'

'Ah. Yes, just a quick aside. I actually own one of your pieces, Daniel. And, Lizzie, it's the one you described, the one you liked. *The Passing of the Thunderstorm* is indeed its title, and I have it on my bedroom wall. I was amazed when you talked of that piece, but I couldn't tell you the reason.'

Lizzie felt a jolt of shocked remembrance. 'Oh! I remember we talked of it. And… you *own* it? Really own it?'

'I do.'

'Okay.' Jake lifted a hand. 'I'm glad we're all into art appreciation. I like Daniel's work, too. Just as well, really. But why are we here, Anton? Why are you telling us we have guests this afternoon? We have guests most afternoons.'

'Not the King and Queen of Mondorra, though,' Anton said calmly.Daniel blinked several times, shaking his head, and Jake and Emily frowned, annoyance growing in their expressions.

'You shouldn't be party to that information,' Emily said coldly.

Anton's eyes narrowed with amusement. 'I am very much party to it because they are my parents.'

The silence which followed was profound.

Claire was the first to break it. 'Bloody hell! Have I been ordering a prince round for the last few months?'

Anton threw back his head and laughed. 'Bea was very approving that I should have a boss, and she was a lady. In our country it is more unusual and something I intend to change. We are behind the times.'

He explained why he was there, the reasons he'd left Mondorra, and the reconciliation which had been started by a letter, continued with the phone call. and would be completed with his parents' visit.

'And I wish to say I am deeply sorry for not explaining who I was maybe from the beginning, but I hope my work has been of satisfaction to Claire.'

Claire looked slightly bemused. 'Oh, I've no complaints about your work. You work hard, and you're good at gardening. But how?'

'My mother is a brilliant gardener, and she takes a great interest in our gardens at home. Hansel is our head gardener and is very clever. I think I take after my mama. I would follow them about when I was young, asking questions. Lots of questions. And if I return home sooner than my promised year, would you accept someone from the palace team to help until you can find another person? Hansel will recommend someone.

And I warn you, Mama will want to see everything about the restoration, including the plans!'

'I'll enjoy showing her round.'

Jake looked serious. 'Emily and I were wondering what we should do, anyway. When they arrive. I'm not a great one for bowing and stuff, but I don't want to piss them off, either.'

Anton let out another shout of laughter. 'They are coming "under the radar" I think they have already said to you? So they want greeting as any other guests, and please, still keep their identity to yourselves so we do not fluster everyone. We are not a big country, but big enough to be invited to weddings linked to your royal family here, which is why they are coming to England. As well, if you mention such titles, people get... excited. They will not want that. Just ordinary guests.'

Anton had received a text after lunch. His parents would arrive around three o'clock. Now, Lizzie stood by his side, her hands trembling, her insides cold, as they stood waiting for them. Yes, she knew, as Anton had kept telling her, she'd met them before, but that was as a famous performer, not as their son's future partner.

'They won't approve,' she muttered, tugging the hem of Anton's tee shirt. 'They wanted you to marry Bea.'

'Are you so very different?'

'I don't know your country. I don't know your customs.'

'You can speak some French? You don't have to know my country—we can explore it, walking, on horseback, by car. Our customs—ah, well, many of those will be slowly changed so I'm glad you are not steeped in them. My mother will love you, and my father will watch you, but I assure you there is nothing he will not like. Calm, my swan princess. This is a stage performance. What do you do then?'

'Deep breathing. Touch the toe of my left ballet shoe and turn round once.' She laughed as she saw one of his eyebrows quirk up and his sideways look.

'Okay. Do it. Now, because I see their car. Look.' He pointed to the top of the drive where a large cream-coloured estate car had just emerged from the avenue of trees, then he glanced behind where Emily and Jake stood ready to welcome them. Emily appeared nervous, but Jake, with a casual arm slung round her shoulders, looked sublimely relaxed.

The car came to a stop. A chauffeur stepped out and opened the door nearest the house, and Anton's supremely elegant and rather beautiful blonde-haired mother stepped out.

Her behaviour didn't match her cool, outward appearance. She rushed forwards and flung her arms round her son, a shine of tears in her eyes as she gave her son a long hug then kissed each cheek before standing back and holding him at arms' length. 'Oh! You look so well! So *happy*. Your tired look has gone, and your down-turned mouth is no more. It's so good to see you!'

A tall man, clearly Anton's father, with dark chestnut hair liberally sprinkled with grey and the same mossy green eyes with gold flecks, stood waiting, and as Anton's mother stepped back, he took her place and hugged his son, also kissing him on both cheeks and slapping him on his back.

Lizzie remembered them, of course she did, but she'd been fearful of Bruno at the time and had felt distanced from events that night, apart from the strange tug to Anton. Or was he now Maximilian? Or Max, as she'd heard Bea call him? Oh, what if his parents looked her up and down and sneered at her? She pulled herself up, tucked in her stomach, her chin lifting.

'Max, my darling, you mentioned you wanted us to meet Lizzie, and told us she is the dancer who came to the palace a year ago.' His mother gave him a gentle reminder because Anton and his father were still gazing at each other, the affection between them clearly visible.

'But of course. Mama, Papa, I would like you to meet Lizzie—Eliza—Cassidy. Lizzie, my parents, Alessandro and Helena de Casimir.' Anton's grip on her arm prevented her curtsey, and she flashed him a surprised look and caught his small head shake. 'I must tell you Lizzie has agreed to marry me.'

Lizzie's stomach lurched most unpleasantly. She surreptitiously wiped her hands down the sides of her jeans and fixed a smile on her face, but she could feel her lips tremble. His parents looked at each other, and his mother give a slight shake of her head. Not, she imagined, in rejection of her, but from what she'd heard of his father, maybe a warning for him to play nice? Not a great start if he was going to be awkward.

Helena took hold of her hands, catching Lizzie by surprise.

'Lizzie, how delightful to meet you again. I can see

you've made my son very happy, and *that* is exactly what we want for him, is it not, Alessandro? To be as happy as we have always been, yes?' She turned her head to look at her husband.

While but Lizzie couldn't see her expression, she heard the tone of her voice which made her smile.

His look changed from a mild glower to a nod, then a smile, and as Helena stepped back, he came forwards to wrap her in a bear hug. 'It is indeed,' he said gruffly. 'Welcome to our family.'

Over his shoulder, she saw Helena smile and nod, and one of Anton's eyebrows rise.

Lizzie felt the tension in her body leach away.

The worst was over.

All would be well. Joy flooded through her. She had recovered her confidence and found love. She had the chance of a further year of dancing internationally before going to Mondorra to set up her own school and maybe one day, her own company, too. She gave a small inward shiver of disbelief at the change from a year ago, and her mind returned to that morning, when they'd stood in the hushed start of a new day. Now she could see everything open up in front of her like the sun rising on a fresh new day, and her heart spilled over and filled her with love, weakening her knees, filling her eyes with tears.

As if sensing her emotion, she found Anton by her side. Always by her side, his hand in hers, his eyes searching her face, checking she was all right.

And she knew it would always be this way. They would be there for each other, for ever.

EPILOGUE

A YEAR HAD PASSED. Haven House Hotel was at its very best. The front of the house now had all the beds restored, and the fountain installed last year was playing, its spray catching the sun and forming rainbows. It was the beginning of July again, and the flower beds were bursting with colour, layer upon layer, from low-growing plants to the higher ones at the back.

The rose garden below the terrace was even more beautiful, and the perfume was stunning, rising into the air from blossoms warmed by the sun. The hotel had lined up the chairs in rows on the terrace and created a bower of roses at the entrance to the rose gardens, which today was doubling as the place where Anton and Lizzie would say their vows. There was to be a formal wedding in Mondorra at the end of the month, but both of them had wanted the real ceremony held here, with the beautiful gardens, the sea a glintingly-blue backdrop, the new fountains adding a counterpoint to the sound of the waves, and all their friends gathered round to witness it.

Dancers from the ballet school were here. Lizzie's sister and husband. Tim. Bea. Anton's parents and some close friends. And of course, Jake and Emily, and Claire and Daniel, as well as Annie, and Jenny. Olivia now had a baby brother who was called Elwyn, and Jamie was soon expecting a baby sister. A small and intimate wedding in the place where they had amazingly found each other and fallen in love.

Their future life would, of necessity, be in Mondorra, but Anton had already effected changes, and the formal court was no more, much to his relief. Other changes had proved immensely popular and were turning Anton into something of a celebrity, but he remained approachable. Lizzie was going to start her ballet school and eventually, a company as well. William had agreed to come and help, and it looked as if Tim would be returning to France at the same time. Although he'd proved a massive success as a ballet dancer over the last year, he'd laughingly said he wanted a return to more varied dancing, but would continue to partner Lizzie occasionally, just to keep his hand in. He and Lizzie had danced together for most of the year since the outreach, with Lizzie flying to Mondorra whenever she had spare time, or Anton coming to England, so they'd spent almost as much time together as apart.

Anton shifted from foot to foot. Every now and again he pushed his hair back from his face. The sighs from Jacques, his personal servant, pleased because these days he had more to do, were audible even above the indistinct murmur of conversation. His best man, a close friend, Joachim, laid his hand on Anton's arm in a soothing gesture.

'Chill, Max. She'll be here. Well, you already know she's here, so unless she does a runner—' He recoiled as Anton glared at him. 'A joke, okay?'

A harpist and violinist from the ballet company's orchestra began to play the pas de deux from Swan Lake.

He turned and saw her approach, her pace slow and stately, in time with the haunting music. She wore a simple gown of cream, the edges trimmed with delicate green and gold embroidery. Dominic accompanied her, and her sister followed behind as maid of honour.

She was breathtaking. She was beautiful. She was ethereal.

And she'd chosen him.

Their eyes met. He stepped forwards and held out both hands.

Handing her flowers to Christina, Lizzie clasped hands with him and gently, their lips met in a butterfly kiss.

The registrar coughed gently. 'You're supposed to kiss the bride *after* the ceremony.'

There was a ripple of laughter among the guests, and Lizzie and Anton turned to make their vows.

Anton had refused the VIP suite. That was for his parents. Instead, after a most delightful reception and dancing, he and Lizzie returned to his room over the garage.

Now, when all lights were out and the guests asleep, she stood in front of him in the room where they'd made love for the first time.

His throat closed as he gazed at her. 'You are so lovely.'

He'd made love to her so many times, now, but each time felt different. Sometimes there was laughter, sometimes grim passion, sometimes tenderness, sometimes sheer, greedy lust. He would never become tired of his swan princess.

'You're not bad, yourself. But let's unwrap you from that suit, shall we?' Delicately, she extended her arms, lifted them above her head, executed a perfect turn before stepping towards him, standing in a meek ballet pose, hands crossed in front of her, feet in position five. But spoiled by the wicked gleam in her eyes, the tongue which slowly licked her lips.

Heat grew. His hands trembled as he undid his tie, shrugged out of his jacket and pulled off the shirt without even undoing more than the top few buttons. When his hands moved to his belt and zip, Lizzie lay hers over his.

'Mine,' she said simply, giving him a wicked grin. 'All mine.'

He stood motionless as she slid her hands up his chest and flicked his nipples before leaning in to suck gently on them. Stepping back, she slowly unbuckled his belt and laughed at the erection pressing against the zip.

'I think you need to come out to play.'

'You,' Anton spoke through gritted teeth, 'are causing me hell, woman!'

She stopped and looked at him from under lowered lashes, her mouth parted. 'Goes both ways,' she murmured, as she slid down the zip and pulled his trousers and boxers down.

Stepping out of them, Anton turned her round and cursed when he saw the many tiny buttons running down the back of her dress. He kissed her shoulder and nipped at her ear as he undid them. 'This dress has been designed to torture bridegrooms,' he muttered. 'I suppose you want to wear it again, and I can't just rip it off you?'

Her only answer was to push against him and move her hips suggestively. It was driving him mad, and if she kept that up, he doubted he'd make it to the bed.

His breath hissed out between his teeth, a combination of frustration with the buttons and the movement of her buttocks against him. 'Lizzie! Stop! I'm begging you. Please remember it's a month since we were together!'

'Oh, I enjoy being begged. Hurry.' Her voice was husky, promising much.

'I'm doing my best!' He couldn't help his laughter at the tone of her voice. 'Hurray! Done.'

Tenderly he turned her to face him and slid the dress off her shoulders and down her body until it pooled on the floor. He followed it until he was on his knees in front of her, her hands fisted in his hair as he kissed her soft stomach, pulled down the wisp of lace covering her, slipped his hand between her legs and found her hot, wet centre.

She bucked under his hand and the time for slow tenderness disappeared as Anton stood, picked her up and carried her to the bed.

Despite it being a hostel room, someone had attempted to turn it into a room fit for a honeymoon couple, with roses, chocolates, champagne, and linen sheets, but they saw none of that. Intent only on each other, on giving and taking pleasure, they were immune to their surroundings.

Anton resumed touching her clit with slow strokes of his fingers and moaned as she took him in her hand and caressed his tip. His feelings built up to an exquisite pressure until it almost became agony, so it was fortunate she climaxed quickly. Her hips rearing up, her hands clenching the sheets, she cried out, his name on her lips. That was his moment, the time he could slip inside her, feel her tightness enclose him, move within her. He grew more and more tense, his muscles and sinews straining as he approached his own climax, aware, Lizzie, too, was reaching for another.

Their cries mingled and subsided. Molten gold replaced his previous tension as he collapsed briefly on top of her before rolling to one side, pulling her to nestle in his arms, kissing her hair, her face her lips as he murmured words of love.

Finally, he drew back and gazed at her, his face serious. 'Oh, my Lizzie...' His throat closed as tears filled his eyes.

'I know,' she replied. 'I know.'

During this last year, they'd gone their own way by necessity. Lizzie had regained her reputation on the international stage as she'd wanted, and Anton, now formally known outside their private quarters as Prince Maximilian, had begun serious talks with industry leaders, women's groups, the Council, and had already achieved so very much regarding infrastructure. They had spoken every day, using video links, now possible since the internet had been updated in Mondorra. Lizzie had visited many times, and they had looked for and decided on a place for her ballet school and negotiated with the theatre where Anton had first seen her perform, to create it as a base for the new company. Brick upon brick, her dreams had risen on a plot behind the theatre and an underground tunnel was built to connect the two.

Now, here, they gazed at each other in awe, that they had achieved their dreams and in front of them saw a contented future where much would be built and much achieved.

They reached out and clasped each other's hands.

'I know,' Lizzie said again.

ACKNOWLEDGMENTS

No book is ever written without input, help and advice from numerous lovely people and the same applies here.

I continue to thank and be very grateful to my editor Whitney Jones, who has helped me enormously and continues to teach me a lot – I shall forever be indebted to her for her kindness and hard work.

Thanks also to Romance Café Publishing for all their support and help in getting this series from its conception to its final form.

Thanks to my lovely beta readers Riana Everly, who picked up on inconsistencies of various kinds and as always, offered excellent constructive criticisms.

An especial mention must go to Riana Everly, for her help with my blurbs.

And last, but not least, thanks to my husband, for tolerating the time I spend writing, for making him listen while I work through an idea and for tolerating my mutterings when something isn't going right.

ALSO BY LIZ MARTINSON

Solhaven Forevers

Love By Sunset

Love By Moonlight

Love By Sunrise

Printed in Poland
by Amazon Fulfillment
Poland Sp. z o.o., Wrocław